Gator Alley

A Chase Gordon Tropical Thriller

Douglas Pratt

MANTA PRESS

Gator Alley is a work of fiction. Any names, places, characters, and incidents are products of the author's imagination or are used fictitiously. Any resemblance to actual persons, either living or dead, events, or locales is entirely coincidental.

Copyright © 2022 by Douglas Pratt

Cover art by

Ryan Schwarz

The Cover Designer

www.thecoverdesigner.com

All rights reserved.

For Ashlee, as always
None of this is possible without you.

In memory of my friend, Sandy Hubbard,
who was always kind, loving, and annoying
in her own special way.

•

ONE

The Mercedes-Benz GLC moved along the hot asphalt southbound on Highway 27, a mixture of sun and clouds overhead. The purr of the engine was smooth, almost silky, like a jazz song. As the tires skirted along the pavement, it resonated like distant thunder. Tinted windows shielded the unrelenting Florida sun.

Audrey Harrod's bare feet crossed at her ankles, resting on the dash. Her lithe toes, lacquered in a soft pink palette, wriggled as she stared at the paperback she'd picked up before leaving Orlando. Folded open, the spine already sported a deep white crease, a feat that Tom never comprehended, given the speed his wife read.

"Do you think we'll see any alligators?" a voice questioned from the back seat.

"You want to see an alligator, Jackson?" Tom Harrod asked his son, glancing into the rearview mirror to see the blond-haired boy staring out the window wistfully.

"Oh yeah," the eight-year-old responded. "I want to count his teeth."

"Count his teeth?" Tom repeated with a grin. Jackson's impetuous nature came from his mother. "The only way to do that is to climb inside his big, open mouth."

Jackson giggled. Even his laughter was a clone of Audrey's, right down to the half snort they both had after a fit.

The boy stifled his mirth, asking, "Did you know that it's easy to hold an alligator's mouth closed?"

"Is it?" Tom questioned without doubting his son's knowledge. The boy had a fascination with animals, but especially reptiles. He'd been begging Audrey for a pet snake for months.

"Yeah, Dad. Even Mom or Amanda could do it."

Audrey lifted her head out of the book. "What do you mean 'even Mom?' You don't think I'm strong enough?" she retorted back to the boy.

"No, Mom," he replied defensively. "You are strong. Just not as strong as us. Isn't that right, Dad?"

Tom shook his head playfully. "Oh, you don't drag me into this. I'm pretty certain your mother would have no trouble whooping my butt."

"Damn straight," she whispered under her breath, so only Tom could hear her.

His white teeth gleamed as he glanced over at his blond wife of nine years. He wanted to comment about how they needed to get the kids into a separate room when they reached the motel tonight. She would grin at him with that lascivious look before rebuffing him. The kids were too young to be in their own room.

"I heard that," Jackson announced, as if he'd just found a hidden trove of treasure. "You said a bad word."

Audrey's eyes cut up to the rearview mirror. "No, I didn't," she lied.

Jackson stared back at her with a blank look, questioning whether to argue with his mother. His face contorted with confusion as he pondered if he should trust his ears or his mother. At his age, he was questioning everything, and the word of either parent was up for dispute.

"How did you like those lions?" Tom asked, shifting the boy's focus back to a less salacious subject.

"They were cool," the boy exclaimed. "Did you see that one daddy one? He was staring at Amanda through the window. I think he wanted to eat her."

"That wouldn't be good," Tom responded.

"I wouldn't've let him," the boy boasted.

"That's right," his father agreed. "What's your job?"

"Protect my sister," he answered bravely. "Your job is to protect all of us."

"And Mom's job?" Tom asked.

"To be pretty." His head lifted high as if he'd just explained some tidbit of physics to a neophyte.

Audrey turned her head sheepishly. "You boys," she remarked with a wide grin that only the mother of a boy seems to have. "What am I going to do with you?"

"Love you, Mom," Jackson told her.

"I love you too, baby," Audrey replied, winking at the kid.

"Looks like Amanda had enough," Tom pointed out.

"Yeah," Jackson chuckled. "She fell asleep after we left the safari place."

They'd broken the trip up into several stops. While Jackson could entertain himself with books and video games, two-year-old Amanda wasn't quite as independent. She'd be three next month, and like most two-year-olds, her attention span was still fairly short. After a long day running from The Pirates of the Caribbean to the Teacups and back to catch the Buzz Lightyear ride, she'd fallen asleep before they made it out of the main gates to the Magic Kingdom. She'd slept all the way to South Florida, where Tom finally pulled into a Holiday Inn. Today's adventure began at seven and carried them through the Lion Country Safari. Both of the kids enjoyed the facade of interaction with the animals, even if the beasts were outside of the car and behind what Tom guessed was a well-hidden electric fence line. At least, he hoped there was some hot wire between the lions and the Mercedes.

Tomorrow, they planned to tour the Everglades with Swamp John's Airboat Tours before continuing south to Key Largo, where they'd spend the rest of the week. Then it was plenty of time in the water. Snorkeling and kayaking were high on his agenda. He cut his eyes over to Audrey, thinking about the bikini he knew she'd packed for the week. Maybe he needed to readjust his agenda.

The dash beeped, and a message flashed across the digital display—Low Fuel. Tom cursed to himself. He had every intention of hitting a gas station just outside the safari park, but Jackson had been talking about whether the lions could fight a velociraptor. The argument lasted over ten minutes, with Jackson's stance that the lions would stand a chance remaining staunch.

"We need to find some gas," Tom remarked absentmindedly.

"I could go for a drink," Audrey responded.

The Mercedes rolled along the highway another four miles before Tom spotted the sign rising in the distance. The price of gas was staggering compared to Tennessee, but he figured in part it was because of the distance the refined fuel had to travel. Most of the oil in the Gulf probably traveled from port cities like New Orleans or Mobile. But honestly, he didn't know. It was just as likely that the gas stations knew Florida was full of tourists looking to drop money wherever they could.

It didn't matter. They didn't travel a thousand miles to worry about the price of gasoline. In the entire scheme of things, Tom realized it was an infinitesimally small first-world problem.

The service station fuel island only had three pumps, and Tom stopped the Mercedes at the last one.

"Dad, can I pump it?" Jackson asked, straining his neck toward the front seat.

"I suppose so," his father acknowledged. "Remember which one to get?"

"Premium, right?" he responded with a hint of doubt in his voice.

"Right," Tom confirmed. "I'll grab us a couple of drinks. Probably hit the head."

Audrey cocked her head to him with a soft, silent rebuke.

He corrected himself. "I mean, I'll use the bathroom."

Audrey smiled contently, and Tom reached over and squeezed her leg just above her knee. He opened the door and climbed out of the Mercedes. Jackson worked quickly to unfasten the buckle on his booster seat. Tom watched as the boy bounced out of the car and grabbed the nozzle.

"Wait a sec," Tom intervened. "I have to put my card in first."

"Oh, sorry, Dad," Jackson offered.

"It's okay," he assured his son. "They just won't start the gas without some money."

Jackson laughed. "It'd be nice if they did," he replied. "We could fill up all the cars."

"The owners of the store might not like that," Tom pointed out.

Jackson nodded as Tom slid his credit card into the slot. "Okay, it's all yours," he informed the boy.

His son didn't waste a second, grabbing the nozzle with both hands and pulling it out the pump.

Tom rubbed the boy's mop of hair as he walked into the convenience store. The door set off a loud ding as he opened it. Inside, the owners hadn't spent a lot of time or money on cleaning. The once-white linoleum floor hadn't seen a mop in months, and it showed grime and stains between the aisles. Tom weaved between a rack of pork rinds and peanuts to the restroom.

Upon immediate inspection, he knew his wife would have turned tail and returned to the car before she'd ever considered using it. Rust corroded through the metal hinges, and the thin metal plates barely held the weight of the door. A rusty spring creaked as he stepped inside. He admitted that at least as a man, he could navigate this literal shithole without touching the toilet.

He finished up, flushing the toilet with his foot to avoid as much contact as possible. Even the sink appeared to have doubled as a urinal more than once. He wasn't much of a germophobe, but this place ranked lower than some latrines he'd dug overseas. Audrey had some hand sanitizer he'd use in the car to ensure he didn't carry any nasty microbes back with him.

The spring screamed as he exited the bathroom. Behind the counter, a greasy-haired blond kid sat on a stool. His head hung over a phone as he slumped forward. A faint odor of weed hung in the air. Tom guessed he'd lit up about an hour earlier, and now the clerk was just reveling in the buzz.

Tom pulled open the dingy glass door and pulled a Diet Coke for Audrey off the rack. His fingers traced along the soda bottles until he found the green Mountain Dew label. He glanced over his shoulder at the kid behind the counter. His phone continued to garner his attention. Tom let the cooler door close, and he went to the next refrigerator, where he pulled a pint of orange juice. He eyeballed the expiration date, not trusting that the staff here rotated their product in a timely manner. Surprised to find it still good, he carried the three drinks to the counter.

The blond head turned up as Tom approached the counter. Glassy blue eyes peered up at him.

"That all?" the kid asked.

Tom set the three bottles on the counter. "Yes."

The echo of the gunshot reverberated through Tom. The second one followed a second later, and Tom's head swiveled toward the door.

Two

The blue skies over South Florida were trying to peek out past the billowing clouds. The afternoon sun was currently hiding behind a threatening storm cloud. My right arm hung out the window. The skies might have appeared gloomy, but the weather was offering a respite from the oppressive heat we'd been dealing with this summer.

Personally, I hate it when people who live in Florida complain about the heat. It was a good portion of the reason I settled here. While this year was exceptionally warm, I would take it over cold and snow any day of the week.

No, I'll take the heat. Besides, no one wears bikinis in the winter.

The twang of Waylon Jennings grew louder as Jay turned up the radio. The threat of rain scared him from removing the top of his Jeep, but he still reveled in the opportunity to push back the front sun visor. He pulled the Ole Miss hat down tight on his head. If the music and attire didn't give away his Mississippi heritage, the slow drawl of the South crawled out with every word. Somehow, he added at least one extra syllable to every word he spoke.

Most of the time, he didn't get three days off in a row. Earlier this year, the department promoted him to Chief Detective for the Palm Beach County Sheriff's Department. I think his head had popped up a total of two days for the first month he had the job. Already, the cracks in his facade were forming. In the Corps, there were plenty of young officers who climbed the ranks to find life at the top sucked. It's a lot of responsibility—scheduling, payroll, counselor. He missed being in the midst of an investigation. Instead, he was answering to the Sheriff about things like crime statistics and case clearance.

This was the first time he'd taken his boat out since the promotion. While it would make sense to grab his gear and take my forty-foot Tartan sailboat out for a long weekend, *Carina* was having some mechanical issues. I burned out a starter, and the local marine store didn't have the right model. It seemed stupid since the plant that manufactured this part was in Miami, but I was getting a part shipped over from Seattle, Washington. For now, my home and escape from the world remained tethered to the dock.

Instead, we towed the 1997 Angler 204 Center Console Jay bought last year. It was ideal for the two of us to take out just about anywhere. This weekend, we tossed a cooler in the boat with a couple of sleeping bags for three days in the Everglades. It was going to be the kind of roughing-it trip neither of us had done since we got out of Afghanistan. Although, this time, we had plenty of beer. Not to mention poles and bait for what should be a thrilling weekend.

"I figure we can get in the water by five, and drop anchor somewhere by dark," Jay mused as he stared ahead.

"We have to make room for the fish," I remarked. "That means drinking some of that beer down."

"No worries, Flash," he replied with a grin. "I got that covered."

We already punched the numbers and estimated a full tank of gas with a five-gallon spare would carry us all over the swamps. The goal wasn't necessarily to get far—just get away. I couldn't agree more. My life was already pretty easy. Since getting out of the Corps, I lived on my boat, picking up a few bartending shifts at the Manta Club. But the last few months had seen me tied to the dock longer than normal. West Palm Beach was beautiful, but it had its drawbacks. Years of developers stacking buildings on top of each other left concrete for as far as the eye could see. The only thing all that concrete accomplished, aside from annihilating ecosystems, was reflecting sun rays. That meant if there was only a slight breeze, the marina was like a marshmallow in a solar oven.

Add to that the light pollution, and I might never lay my eyes on a constellation if I stayed in port. At least when I fell asleep tonight, there would be nothing but glittering stars shining down on me.

Jay's phone buzzed, and he glanced at the screen before dropping it back into the console. His face contorted slightly, as if he felt a slight discomfort.

"Everything good?" I asked.

"Yeah, it's my brother again," he remarked. "Dad apparently wandered off for six hours the other day. He found him in the casino over in Biloxi. He was just sitting at a slot machine for an hour. Didn't even play the damn thing. Just staring at the lights."

"Think it's some kind of dementia?" I asked.

Jay shrugged. "I don't know. Teddy wants me to come back. You know, to help keep an eye on him."

It wasn't a quandary I was going to have. My own father sat in prison for killing my brother. The only reason I'd consider going back to face him was to put a bullet in his head. Although, even that was more attention than I thought Gerald Gordon deserved.

The Jeep slowed as the speed limit changed from forty-five miles per hour to thirty-five. We were far enough inland that the view along the highway was nothing but stretches of dilapidated businesses and service stations. On the side of the road, I counted six pop-up shops manned by Latino women with two or three kids running around playing. Balloons and flowers seemed to be the main commerce. All of it came from the same factory—cheap junk these women were trying to hock to feed the kids. This was the only honest work these people could find. I didn't know whether they were legal immigrants. It was a fair bet that most didn't speak English well enough to find other work, especially with children to care for. Somehow, the media still found ways to vilify them.

"You're thinking about it?" I asked.

"What?"

"Going back to Mississippi," I clarified. "You feel guilty about not being there."

"Yeah," he remarked. "But I just got the promotion here. What would I do?"

As I considered a sarcastic quip, Jay braked as he pulled off the road into a service station. Whatever quick comeback I had formed in my head vanished.

"Jay!" I exclaimed, pointing to the gas pumps.

The Jeep lurched to a halt, thrusting me against the seat belt. We both bounded out of the car.

"He took my car!" a short, older woman hollered.

Jay pulled his service gun from the holster on his belt, and I ran toward the two figures lying on the concrete.

What lay before me wasn't the most gruesome I'd witnessed, but it was bad. The first body I reached was a young boy, maybe seven or eight years old. When the round struck him, it mauled his face, leaving a disfigured visage. I doubt he registered the gunshot before he was dead—a relief in some respects.

The other corpse belonged to a woman in her early thirties. Mom. Judging from the sprawled position, I guessed she heard the boy get shot, jumped out of the car, and took a round to the chest. She was wearing leggings and a t-shirt. The paperback lying on the ground was an adventure novel—the kind one might read on a road trip or vacation. She was barefooted, as if she'd slipped her shoes off while riding along—more comfortable.

"Oh shit," Jay murmured as he came up behind me. "Clerk said it was a carjacking."

I glanced at the gas pump. The nozzle hung loosely where the boy had dropped it. Just over twenty-two gallons.

"There's a father," Jay informed me. "We just missed him by a few seconds. He took the old woman's car and went after the killers."

"Damn," I whispered, staring at the bodies on the ground.

"I'm calling the Miami-Dade Police. The Chief Detective over there knows me," Jay told me.

As I nodded, my eyes drifted to the road. The father was in pursuit. What was going to happen when he caught them?

It was understandable. The family was on a road trip—probably heading to the Keys or the Everglades National Park. Dad goes inside to pay or maybe just hit the bathroom when someone comes along and kills his wife and son. That kind of grief and rage can drive even the average man to vengeance.

Jay was on his cell phone, and I'd seen enough of the victims for them to pop up in my dreams for years to come. I walked toward the store where the old woman who I now took a few seconds to study was pacing nervously.

"Are you hurt, ma'am?" I asked, assuming Jay had already done the same.

"It's so horrible," she muttered, wiping a bead of sweat from her face and smearing the heavy mascara on her eyes.

"Why don't we step inside out of the heat?" I asked. While the clouds were still shielding us from the sun, they rarely abated the Florida heat completely. But this woman's perspiration was likely a result of stress more than temperature.

"Do you think I could get a bottle of water?" she asked, taking my hand as I guided her into the store.

"Yes, I'm sure we can take care of that," I assured her.

"I hope that poor man is okay," she stated.

"The one who took your car?"

She nodded. "I don't want him to get in any trouble," she insisted. "He just watched someone kill his wife and son."

"Did you see it happen?" I asked.

She shook her head. "When I pulled in, he ran out of the store with a gun and took my car. He told me he was sorry."

"He had a gun?" I questioned.

"Yeah," the clerk behind the counter answered. "He took the shotgun I keep behind the counter."

That tidbit of information seemed to change things. I wondered if Jay knew that yet. It wouldn't matter, really. This wasn't his county,

and he had no jurisdiction. But Jay would re-
lay any information to the Miami-Dade officers
when they got here.

I looked over at the clerk. "Can this woman
get a bottle of water?" I asked.

He responded with a nod, and I walked to the
back of the store where a row of coolers lined
the wall. When I returned with a cold water,
I helped the woman into a booth where cus-
tomers could enjoy their hot dogs or whatever
food people ate in a gas station.

"What happened?" I asked the clerk.

The clerk was in his twenties, with stringy
blond hair and a pockmarked face. When he
spoke, it was obvious he was missing several
teeth.

"Guy came in to get some drinks," he explains,
pointing at three bottles on the counter—a Diet
Coke, an orange juice, and a Mountain Dew.
"His kid was filling up. Man had just put the
drinks up here when we heard the first shot. By
the time he turned toward the door, there was
a second shot, and the car took off."

"What did you do?"

"Grabbed my shotgun and ran after him. He
went to his family. When he realized they were
dead, he stood up and came back toward me.
He wanted to view the footage."

"The footage?" I asked.

The clerk stuck a finger in the air at the camera over the counter. "Security."

"Did you call 911?"

"Dude was insistent," he argued defensively.
"Scary, man."

I didn't scold the kid for not calling the cops. It probably wouldn't have mattered to the boy and his mother at that point.

"Did he watch the video?"

The clerk nodded.

Jay came into the store. "Miami-Dade is going to send a car, but they have a hostage situation at a trailer park on the north side of the county. I told Steve, the Chief Detective, I'd secure the scene until his guys get here."

"What kind of hostage situation?" the clerk asked.

Jay shrugged.

"Let's see the video," I suggested.

"I don't think that's a good idea," Jay responded.

"The father watched it before he left," I explained. "He took the gun from behind the counter."

"Great," Jay retorted. "He's armed."

I nodded.

He looked at the clerk. "Play the video."

The clerk moved to two monitors behind the counter. One showed six camera angles while the other displayed a full screen angle of the cash register. He tapped a few keys and moved the mouse around on the monitor. The video started. It seemed weird to realize the entire incident took place less than eight minutes ago. We watched the car at the pump as the boy filled the tank. He rocked back and forth on each leg in an almost dance. He seemed to talk to himself as he pulled the nozzle out of the car.

A figure appeared on the screen. It was a Latino man, probably not even twenty. He raised a Hi-Point nine-millimeter toward the kid and fired point blank. The mother jumped out of the car, but another figure came toward her and fired another pistol. I couldn't distinguish the make or caliber, but I guessed a nine or a forty-five. The two teens jumped into the front seat and peeled away from the pumps.

"Stop it," I demanded.

The clerk complied.

"Back it up a second or two," I ordered.

"What's that?" I asked, tapping my finger on the screen where the camera's angle seemed to look right through the back window.

"A car seat," Jay answered.

"That kid might have been in a booster seat," I pointed out.

"There's another kid in the car," Jay announced.

THREE

J ay pulled his phone out and frantically dialed a number.

"Steve, it's Jay Delp again. You need to issue an Amber Alert. There was another child in the car that was jacked."

He stepped outside as he rattled off the vehicle's description. My attention returned to the two monitors. The monitor with six angles showed the story as it played out. As the Mercedes peeled away from the pumps, the father ran into the camera's view. He paused a microsecond as he moved past his son. When he reached his wife, he dropped to his right knee.

Something tickled the back of my brain.

He held the woman's hand for a second before he pulled her wedding ring off her finger. Then he brushed his hand across her cheek before rising to his feet. The man marched back toward the front of the store. For a second, he vanished from one camera before appearing on the camera covering the store's front door. The clerk cradled a sawed-off twelve-gauge shotgun—illegal in the state but effective. The father grabbed it from the clerk's hands and said something to the employee. No, he didn't say something. He barked an order, and the clerk walked back around the counter to the video monitors.

That tickle in my brain grew stronger.

The father paused in his tracks. His eyes drifted to the three bottled drinks that were sitting on the counter before he stared straight up at the camera.

That tickle was no longer just a little nuisance. It became recognition. I knew the man's face.

I'm not some savant with eidetic memory. His face didn't pop up in some mental database automatically.

Instead, it hung there like a giant question mark.

One thing I was certain of—this man wasn't someone I'd met while behind the bar. There were a lot of faces that came at me while I was bartending, but this man wasn't one of them. His response was the giveaway.

Everyone has their own method for dealing with trauma. Some break down immediately. Others panic. Then there are those that react. This man reacted, but not in the typical manner one expects of someone who'd just lost his wife and son. The only emotion he let go was less than five seconds as he squatted beside his wife's body.

He experienced death. More than once. He was military—the ones that lost brothers in battle. The wedding ring. It was like he was pulling dog tags off a fallen comrade. That was the type of thing one did when they realized they couldn't guarantee they'd get the body back.

"Did he pay for the gas?" I asked the clerk.

"Yeah," he responded.

"Credit card?"

The man examined the screen on the register before nodding.

"I don't suppose it tells you his name?"

He stared at the screen, reading, "Thomas Harrod."

The name didn't ring any bells. Usually, a name would trigger something.

"Can you replay it?" I asked.

The replay began, showing the boy pumping gas. He'd pulled the nozzle free of the car when the figure showed up.

"Pause it," I ordered. When the clerk obeyed, it occurred to me he likely assumed I was a cop, too. I didn't dissuade him. Instead, I leaned close to the monitor to study the image. The shooter was a Latino kid. I call him a kid, but he was at least nineteen or twenty. He wore a snapback hat with a Miami Dolphins logo. He wore a long-sleeved t-shirt and black jeans. On the back of the hand holding the gun was a tattoo of an alligator head with a snakelike body vanishing beneath his sleeve. Another bit of ink tried to peek over his collar, but from this angle it was impossible to distinguish.

"Can you print that?" I asked.

The clerk stared at me blankly. "It's not connected to a printer," he commented in a confused and condescending tone. "I can send it to your phone."

"I don't have a phone," I remarked.

His brow furrowed. It was the same confused expression everyone got when they realized I didn't tether myself to the rest of the world. However, the fact he presumed I was a cop made it into a bigger deal. What kind of cop doesn't have a cell phone with him?

"We were going fishing," I explained. "I forgot it."

The excuse still confused him. Most people panic at even the notion of being away from their phone for any length of time, but, like everyone, he'd no doubt left his phone before. It wasn't an uncommon occurrence, but it still slowed him down.

"Tell you what," I suggested. "Send it to my partner's phone." I gave him Jay's number, and he typed a few keystrokes.

"Can you get a screenshot of the dad's face?" I asked. "When he looks directly into the camera?"

He shrugged.

"Do you expect he caught up to those people?" the woman at the booth asked.

I glanced over at her. Her frail fingers fiddled with the label on the bottle of water. Through the wire-framed bifocals, she stared past the bottle. The initial shock was wearing off. That adrenaline rush subsided, and emotions bubbled up. Maybe she had grandkids or great-grandchildren at the same age as that young boy. Grandmothers shouldn't outlive their grandchildren. It happens every day, but that so-called truth has made a permanent nest in our psyches.

"Let's hope not," I responded to her.

"I guess he'd kill them," the clerk blurted out.

"Or the other way around," I retorted.

Jay came back through the door. As the bell on the entrance dinged, the distant sound of sirens slipped through the door.

"He sent you a couple of images," I explained to Jay before glancing at the clerk. "What's your name again?" I asked, knowing he hadn't given it to me.

"Brandon," he answered.

Jay pulled his phone out, looking at the two pictures. "What is this?" he asked, staring at the tattoo on the shooter's arm.

"I hoped you might recognize it," I told him. "Could be a gang tattoo."

"Looks familiar," he noted. "I'll forward it to Steve—Detective Arwoods. Once the unis show up, I'll hand it off to them."

He flipped to the next picture and stared for several seconds at the face of Thomas Harrod. His eyes cut up to me. I saw the same recognition on his face. If Jay recognized Harrod, then it certainly narrowed the field to people we'd come in contact with during the service.

His head motioned me toward the door. I followed him outside.

"Who is this?" he asked. "The face is familiar, but I can't pinpoint it."

"Me too," I replied. "I couldn't place him. But when I watched the video, he moved or,

rather, reacted methodically. Everything about
it screamed ops training."

The sirens were blaring down the street, and
we both turned to watch a patrol car bounce
into the drive of the service station. The flashing lights vanished for a second as the cruiser
passed behind Jay's Jeep. They reappeared as
the officer slammed the car into park and exited
the vehicle.

The other officer opened the passenger door
and stepped out with his hand resting on his
forty-five-caliber service piece. "You Detective
Delp?" the officer asked.

"Yes," Jay replied, pulling his badge out for the
deputies.

The driver walked behind his vehicle toward
the two bodies. "Dispatch said there's a missing
child too?" he asked as he sucked in air through
his teeth.

"We presume so. The surveillance video
shows a car seat in the car. We can't be sure
there was a child in it. However, it was too small
for the boy."

The other officer stepped closer. A yellow
patch on his brown uniform declared his last
name was Clatch. He asked, "The father?"

"He took the clerk's shotgun and stole another customer's vehicle to give pursuit."

"Damn!" Clatch mumbled. "How long ago?"

"About fifteen minutes," Jay responded.

"Who are you?" the driver asked me.

"Chase Gordon," I responded. "I'm with Chief
Delp." I realized his title wasn't actually Chief,
but he was the Chief of Detectives, and it served

him better if these two recognized he was the one they should look to.

The driver seemed to ignore me. "How long have you been here?" he asked Jay.

"We pulled in about ten minutes ago."

"Eleven, technically," I corrected him. "It was 3:27, according to the clock on the dash."

The driver stared at me. I took a glance at his uniform to read his name—Clark. "What was the make and model of the vehicle the child is in?" he asked.

"It was a Mercedes SUV. One of those hatch-back looking ones," Jay explained. "Black. It was the GLC model. I'd need to watch the video a little closer again."

"Dispatch says they'll have a detective coming soon, but there's an incident," Clatch told him. "The Chief of Detectives is on his way, but until then, we answer to you."

"Let's get that Amber Alert out. We need to get a description of the second vehicle out. I'd suggest getting word to surrounding counties. We are pretty close to Miami-Dade, Monroe, and Collier."

"Yes sir," Clatch responded.

As Clatch returned to his vehicle to send word to his dispatcher, Jay pointed Clark toward the bodies. "Until your crime scene people get here, keep that area clear of anyone that might show up. This is still a busy enough street to create an issue."

"He was in boot with us," Jay told me. His change in direction caught me off guard. I'd been listening to him bark orders to the deputies, and when he directed his comment to me, I was off-focus.

"Sorry, I'm blanking," I responded. "Pretty certain that I'd remember him if he passed through boot with us."

"Shit," Jay mumbled. "What was his name? Calvin?"

My brow furrowed as I tried to remember. "Wait!" I blurted out. "Caleb something. Wasn't that it?"

"Yeah, Caleb," Jay confirmed as he nodded. "He bailed or something after a few weeks."

I remembered the guy now. It was strange how the instant the dots connected in my brain, it all flooded back to me. He spent a couple of weeks with us before he just wasn't there. No one acted like he'd gone AWOL. The response was uncommon for that kind of disappearance, and it usually made an excellent object lesson for the rest of the grunts. Wherever Caleb landed, no one ever mentioned him. When you are a couple of young grunts being ground down to dust, the last thing you do is ask your CO why someone isn't there. Instead, I pushed Caleb out of my mind.

Until today.

"His credit card said Thomas Harrod," I commented.

"Alias?" Jay pondered. "Could be a brother."

I considered the way he moved on camera. It was unlikely that this would be a brother to someone we were both acquainted with a long time ago. In the back of my mind, a mental tidbit nudged its way forward.

"On the video," I remarked. "Before he stole that woman's car, he looked at the camera. It was like he realized someone was going to recognize him."

"What do you mean?" Jay questioned.

"It was resignation on his face. He looked at the drinks he'd put on the counter and then he stared for a full second at the camera. I believe he realized he just gave away his identity."

"He's on the run?"

"I'm just guessing here, Jay," I admitted. "It felt weird."

"Damn, what was his last name?" Jay implored.

"You could run his prints," I advised.

"That would take too long," he pointed out. "He's on a direct heading for these gang-bangers."

I shrugged. "I can't blame him," I said. "They killed his family and probably have his kid. I'd burn down everything between here and Key West to get them."

Jay stared at me for a second. "I know what you are thinking, Flash."

I shook my head. "He's trying to save his kid."

"We think he is," Jay corrected me. "There's no actual proof there's another kid in the car."

"What if it were me?" I asked.

"That's a little different," he pointed out.

"We don't really know what happened to Caleb," I added. "Someone could have transferred him to San Diego. If I recall, he was a natural. It would be safe to assume he made the cut."

"He was a dead-shot," Jay remarked.

It might have been the innate talent Caleb had that kept him in the back of our minds. Most of us came in with some experience with weapons of some sort. Even the die-hard hunters who seemed to have started right out of the womb were literally hit or miss. However, Caleb could put a round in the middle of every target no matter what gun he touched.

"We need to go after him," I implored.

"I have to stay here," Jay insisted. "At least until Miami-Dade gets more people here."

I looked at him. We both knew time was wasting. Caleb had over a quarter of an hour's head start on us. The longer we waited, the less chance we had of finding him before he walked into whatever he was chasing.

Jay's face twisted. "You need to get a phone," he demanded. "And keep the damn thing on you."

FOUR

Alonzo "Lonzo" Wilson squeezed the steering wheel with a death grip. If he let up at all, the fingers would tremble. As it was, he had to remind himself to breathe slowly, otherwise his chest would heave as he huffed and puffed through the adrenaline. Without glancing at Gaspar, he wondered if the twenty-two-year-old was reacting the same way.

Lonzo didn't think so. Gaspar had been part of *Las Serpientes* for a few years. This wasn't his first jacking.

But for Lonzo, it was. It was his ride-or-die moment.

He kept seeing the kid's face right before he shot it. When he finally decided to do it, Lonzo gritted his teeth and charged forward. He had already committed to pulling the trigger before he looked into the kid's eyes.

The gunshot was louder than he expected. Sure, he'd fired guns plenty of times before, but this one was just louder.

He watched the kid's face explode. The gas nozzle had drifted down like a feather to the ground, followed by the boy's limp body. When

Gaspar shot the woman, it only sounded like
a pop. Lonzo's ears were still ringing from his
own gun, though.

They'd sat down the street for an hour waiting for the right car. As soon as Lonzo spotted the Mercedes, he knew Gaspar would push
him for it. The thought of killing someone
didn't scare him, even if this was his first time.
If anything, he was more afraid of not doing
it. He'd been running with *Las Serpientes* for a
few months—selling smack and crank, running
lookout. If he wanted more, he had to prove
he was a *Serpiente*. He'd made the mistake of
getting the ink on his arm, thinking it would
prove it to Xavier and the others. That only
pissed them off. Gaspar pulled him to the side.
The message was simple—time to nut up.

That meant laying it on the line. *Las Serpientes*
weren't pussies, Gaspar explained. They were
killers.

Luckily, it didn't matter who the first was. It
was just a proving ground.

Lonzo didn't like the feeling, though. He remembered the boy's eyes. They didn't know
what was coming.

It continued to loop through his head. He
marched a beeline toward the car. As he made
the last six steps, he raised the nine. The kid
must have heard him or something. He turned
to face Lonzo, and Lonzo squeezed the trigger.
Next came the screech of the mother, followed
by a single pop from Gaspar's gun. Lonzo slid
into the driver's seat as Gaspar stepped over the

dead woman and jumped into the passenger's side.

The aroma of burning rubber and gunpowder lingered around Lonzo. They had ten miles to go to the garage, where he'd hand off the Mercedes to one of Xavier's guys. They'd strip it or sell it. Lonzo didn't know what they'd do with it. He figured it was a fifty-thousand-dollar car. Maybe it was closer to a hundred thousand. Whatever it cost was more than any car Lonzo had ever driven.

"You did good, man," Gaspar announced, breaking the silence.

"Yeah, I did," Lonzo affirmed, despite the sweating palms and racing heartbeat.

"The first time is a fucking rush," Gaspar explained. "You'll get used to it."

"Really?" he asked. "I can't get my chest to stop pounding."

Gaspar laughed. "It's awesome. Did you see that bitch as she came toward you?"

"No," Lonzo admitted. "She screamed something, though."

"Bitch's face was priceless when she saw me there," he howled, laughing. "Pop, pop, pop."

Lonzo didn't correct him. He'd only shot once. The pop still rang in his ears. She screamed and bang.

"You ain't no virgin no more," Gaspar cackled. "You gotta celebrate. We need to get some twisters and get fucked up tonight."

"Gotta get the ride to Xavier first," Lonzo pointed out.

"Xavier ain't gonna be there," Gaspar insisted.

Lonzo shook his head. He didn't want to be in this car any longer than he had to. If a cop pulled him over, they'd nail him for murder. Best to dump this thing with whoever Xavier wanted him to and then go blow off some steam.

"No way, man," Lonzo stated. "Xavier said, 'drop the ride off,' I'm gonna drop it off."

"Whatever, man," Gaspar mumbled, pulling his phone out. "I'll still set us up with some girls. You think you can get it up now?"

Lonzo cut his eyes over to his partner. "Hell yeah."

Gaspar's eyebrows lifted knowingly. "You'll be pounding extra hard tonight," he acknowledged.

Lonzo didn't want to admit it, but the idea of doing anything felt alien to him. Oh, he'd follow Gaspar's lead—anything else was a weakness. *Las Serpientes* didn't cower. They didn't worry about anything outside of the *Serpientes*. They certainly didn't dwell on the eyes of some kid.

If Gaspar thought he was doing otherwise, he might tell Xavier. He had to stay in motion.

Lonzo was on autopilot, though. He paid no attention to the yellow lines in the middle of the road racing past. His subconscious kept the wheels of the Mercedes from crossing over the line. Everything else was trying to push the eyes of the boy out of his head. The kid didn't have time to beg for his life. Lonzo doubted he even knew what was coming. But he still saw the eyes. The blast from the nine left everything ringing, but Lonzo's imagination was filling in the gaps. The thud as the kid's head struck the asphalt. He wondered if it was a dull sound or had the brains and blood given it a more squishy sound as it impacted.

His right hand slipped off the steering wheel. The fingers touched the cell phone in his right pants pocket. Lonzo wanted to check the news. Had anyone reported it yet? Surely, the gas station attendant called the cops immediately. What about the father? He was a big guy, Lonzo noted. They had watched him go into the store. What was he doing right now? Staring at his dead family?

Bile seeped up from his gut. Lonzo swallowed hard, forcing the acid back down. Don't throw up, he thought. That wasn't an option. As if it wasn't bad enough to have Gaspar watch him lose his shit, he'd be leaving all sorts of DNA in the car. Couldn't the cops test for that kind of thing in puke? It seems like he saw something like that on whatever cop show his *abuela* was watching once.

"Mama," a voice called from behind him.

Lonzo jerked around with Gaspar to stare in the back seat. A blond-haired girl stared back at them from a car seat.

"Where's Mama?" the child asked, sucking in air with desperation.

"There's a fucking kid in here," Gaspar muttered.

Lonzo turned back to watch the road. He swallowed hard as more acid flooded his throat.

"We gotta get rid of her," Gaspar exclaimed.

Lonzo spun his head toward his partner. "She's a baby!" he argued.

"Man, we can't keep her," Gaspar retorted. "Xavier'll kill us."

He pulled the forty-five out of his pants, and Lonzo grabbed his arm. "No!" he demanded. "We aren't killing her."

"Seriously, you're going to worry about this now. We already killed her brother."

"Shut up, Gaspar," Lonzo ordered. "You'll scare her."

"I ain't worried about scaring the little bitch," he howled, trying to turn toward the back seat.

"You'll ruin the seats," Lonzo pointed out desperately.

Gaspar rolled his eyes as he considered what killing the child would do. Lonzo cringed at the image flashing through his head, and he held back the sigh of relief he felt when Gaspar pulled the forty-five back to the front seat and faced forward.

"We have to do something with her," he pointed out.

Lonzo nodded, but he knew he couldn't kill her. In fact, he wouldn't let Gaspar kill her.

"She's just a baby," Lonzo commented. "She can't identify us. Just don't look at her again so she won't recognize your face."

Gaspar stretched his torso so he could slide the barrel of the forty-five into his waistband. "Xavier's going to shit a brick," he mumbled.

"No names," Lonzo suggested under his breath.

The passenger folded his arms and slouched down, pouting. "Just get us to the garage," he moaned to Lonzo. "I'll send..." He paused before mentioning Xavier's name again. "I'll send a message about our situation."

Lonzo nodded. His eyes cut to the rearview mirror to see the scared pale face staring back. The girl's eyes were wet, and he suspected it wouldn't take long for the tears to come.

As if on command, the baby released a wail. Gaspar slapped his palm on the dash and glared at Lonzo.

FIVE

My right hand rested on top of the steering wheel as I held the needle of the speedometer so that it quivered just under fifty miles per hour. With the boat dragging behind me, I didn't want to go much faster. Cold air rushed from the vents, chilling my knuckles as I held the Jeep between the double yellow line and the narrow shoulder.

There was no way to know what direction Caleb or Thomas or whatever he called himself took. The surveillance video showed him taking the keys from the old lady in what might have been the most polite manner. Even the woman admitted he was apologetic and sad. He sped southwest in the old lady's gray Chevy Nova. It didn't seem likely he'd have a clue where to go, either. But his determination clearly shone through on camera.

My memories of Caleb were fairly vague. He was there, and one day he wasn't. Of course, that time of my life couldn't be defined as my most observant. Those first few weeks as a boot basically put me into survival mode. Everything blended together. While our rotation meshed, we were all so self-involved with not failing. I didn't even get to develop a friendship with Jay until after the Corps deployed us together. Those weeks comprised nothing more than the constant wearing down everything in me until they exhausted me. Every day continued to repeat. And one day I realized that whoever Chase Gordon had been before he reached Parris Island had died. I was completely different.

Despite what happened to Caleb between those days and now, there was reason to think he and I weren't that different. If I were in his shoes, I had to consider what I would do. My wife and son were murdered, and the killers escaped with my baby in the back seat of my car.

I'd kill them. Simple. Nothing in the world allowed them to live past today.

But first and foremost, I had to find them.

I did not know what Caleb would try, but unless he had information I wasn't privy to, it would require someone telling him where they were.

The two carjackers were in a fairly new Mercedes. By now, they'd assume the cops were called, so they'd need to get rid of it quick. Everything about the way they acted indicated they planned this. Probably staked out the gas station for hours until the right ride pulled in. Even then, they waited until the only threat disappeared inside the store. Not that it was the deftest of plans, but it showed a certain level of intent. This wasn't just a joyride. Those two were shopping for the right car.

If that was the case, what did they plan to do with the car now?

The answer seemed to be getting it off the street. What was the going rate for a stolen Mercedes? It had to be a few thousand. It was easy to assume they already had a place to drop it. But where?

Jay could probably find a list of potential chop shops, but it would take time. Not to mention it would put Caleb in the crossfire.

Before I left the gas station, I took Jay's advice, grabbing a prepaid cell phone from the rack. Now I dialed a Miami number and waited as it rang.

"Padrino's," a young female voice answered.

"May I speak with Julio Moreno?" I asked.

"Uh..." the girl responded. "Hold on, please."

There was a slight rustle of noise, followed by an echoing hollowness coming from the phone. One doesn't call the biggest drug lord in the Southeast, ask for him by name, and not expect there to be some confusion. The poor hostess at Padrino's wasn't expecting it. No one called Julio Moreno directly. He conducted business through intermediaries and lackeys. The Cuban restaurant in South Miami was his home base, but as far as the average onlooker would suspect, he was little more than a restaurateur. And Tony Soprano was a garbage man, right?

"Who are you wishing to speak with?" a gruff accent asked, interrupting my thought.

"Julio Moreno, please," I repeated.

"Who is this?"

"Tell him Chase Gordon would like to speak to him."

"Gordon," the voice repeated, and I recognized the intonation as my name came through the speaker.

"Esteban," I exclaimed. "You are the next best thing."

"What do you want, Gordon?" the enforcer questioned.

Esteban Velasquez was Julio Moreno's number two man. When I first met him, we didn't exchange pleasantries. Instead, he tried to kill me, and I didn't particularly like that idea. So I didn't let him. In my mind, I'll always refer to him as Scar, a pseudonym I attached to him based on the jagged scar going down his face. Since our first encounter, I've grown somewhat attached to the little sociopath. Of course, I say "little" when the enforcer loomed over six feet tall like a brick wall with fists.

Really, though, we seemed to have a mutual respect for each other. While Julio Moreno had attempted on more than one occasion to employ me in some fashion, I'd skirted around him without offending him enough to kill me. Jay has warned me, though, that each time I pass near him I'm like Icarus soaring toward my doom. He's right too, but for the moment, I find Esteban and Julio Moreno to be more useful than threatening.

"I'm looking for some people," I explained.

"Try the phone book," Scar snipped.

"Cute," I replied. "No one has a phone book anymore."

"Who do you want to find?" he questioned.

"About half an hour ago—closer to forty minutes by now—there was a carjacking at a gas station on Highway 997."

"Why would you call me about a carjacking?" Scar interrupted.

Shaking my head, I retorted, "If you'll let me finish. There were two kids who shot a mother and her son and stole a Mercedes. I think it was a GLC or something like that. There's a baby in the car."

A grunt emanated from the phone, and I assumed he was still listening to me.

"Obviously, time is of the essence. I need to find where they might take the car. The closest chop shop."

"Do I fucking look like a mechanic, Gordon?" he growled.

"Of course not," I told him, trying to play nice since I needed something from him. "But these kids looked like they belonged to some gang, and I thought with your expertise, you might point me in the right direction."

"I don't have anything to do with those things," he stated, but I doubted that was completely true. He didn't have any gang affiliations now, but I guessed when he was younger, it was nearly mandatory in his community to find a side to stand with.

"Listen, this is a big ask," I admitted. "I just want a direction."

Scar sighed into the phone. "What can you tell me about them?"

"They were both Latino. I couldn't tell you if they were Cuban, Mexican, or what."

"Yeah, yeah, yeah," Velasquez muttered. "We all look alike to the *gringos*."

I ignored his remark, mainly because I didn't have an answer to it. To some extent, he was correct, and while I didn't want that to be true, I knew I had no argument for myself. "One had a snake tattoo. It was hard to see, but it seemed to be on his arm and the back of his hand."

"Black?" he asked. "With fangs?"

"I think so," I answered.

"How old?"

"Mid-twenties at best. Could be younger."

"Mmmm," he mused. "Let me get back to you."

"Do you need this number?" I asked.

"We have caller ID," he commented.

"Of course," I said as he hung up on me.

My speed crept up to sixty, and I glanced in the rearview mirror, surprised because I forgot I had a boat trailing along behind me. I considered calling Jay with an update, but I didn't really have an update, and if I told him I'd called Scar for information, his face would get this disapproving countenance.

Instead, I dialed another number from memory. If the man I was chasing down the highway was Caleb, I wanted to understand why he was going by the name Thomas Harrod. What happened to him?

The number I called belonged to General Judith Shaw. Before she was overseeing some clandestine department at the Pentagon, she was mine and Jay's commanding officer. Before I got out of the Corps, she moved to the Pentagon and soon got her first star. Had I stayed with the Marines, I'd have likely followed her. Despite my loyalty to her and the Corps, I realized it wasn't something I wanted to do. I'd put in my years, and with the help of the Temporary Early Retirement Authority, I pursued the boat bum life afforded to me in my new civilian life.

While Shaw might have never commanded Caleb, I hoped she had the power to pull a few strings and find out what happened to him. There was something about his sudden reappearance that bugged me. It niggled at the back of my brain, prodding me with questions.

The phone rang four times before a young male answered. "General Shaw's office."

"Is the General in?" I asked.

"No, sir," the grunt answered, without knowing whether I was a superior.

"Do you know when she'll be back?" I asked.

"She has a meeting at fifteen hundred hours, sir."

"Can you have her call Lieutenant Chase Gordon at this number?" I asked.

"What's the number?" he questioned.

"You don't have caller ID?"

"No, sir."

I gave him my number and hung up, wondering at the irony that a drug lord can identify a caller faster than the Pentagon. It's reasons like this that America is losing the war on drugs.

SIX

A little auburn-colored house sat squarely on the block in front of him. Nestled at the end of a run-down cul-de-sac, the yard was filled with sand and rock, enclosed by sagging, rusting chain-link fence. Thirty years ago, the house might have been a cozy middle-class home where servicemen stayed off-base. A few years after that, it might have been a cheaper first home for a starter family needing only a small share of TLC. Now, the front porch sported the same peeling paint as the rest of the house. Several lapboards had long since gone missing, either torn from the side or disintegrated with years of rot. Takeout bags and beer cans littered the small yard.

Tom watched the orange house as a small-framed Latina woman at the cottage next door carried a basket full of clothes to lay across the fence line. The graying hairs filtered through the former jet-black head, allowing Tom to guess her age at around fifty. As she stretched t-shirts and shorts out for the sun to warm, her head swiveled toward the same house. Behind her, two small kids—boys—ran around the yard, chasing each other. They were a couple of years younger than Jackson was.

Was. He repeated the word in his head as he watched the children. Was. Jackson was.

His gut tightened, recalling the form of his little boy sprawled on the ground next to the gas pump's nozzle. The image seared into his mind. Bile climbed up the back of his throat, and he forced it back.

Why hadn't he pumped the gas? If he'd have just filled up after the safari park, this wouldn't have happened.

Stop it, he cursed himself. Recriminations were pointless, he reminded himself.

Combat should have taught him that. There is no time to worry or blame during a battle.

This wasn't a target or even a fellow soldier. It was his eight-year-old son. Jackson wasn't charging after U.S. troops with a rusted assault rifle. He'd been pumping gas because he wanted to be a "big boy."

No, he realized. There had been nothing in his past to prepare him for this. No fight he had ever been in left him holding the dead body of his son or his wife. Nothing could take that feeling away from him. He couldn't understand the rage and despair he was experiencing right now.

Focus, he ordered himself.

His eyes narrowed as he scanned the street in front of him. A door opened on the side of a house to his left, and he knew he found his target.

A young Latino boy in his late teens sauntered out of the house, shouting something in Spanish over his shoulder. Crude tattoos appeared to be hand drawn on his arms. The door slammed behind him as he shoved it closed with a force that eventually would tear the screen door from its hinges.

He strolled toward an old Honda Del Sol that had once been cherry red. Now the faded paint left white speckles all over the now-dulled finish. Under the gray shirt hanging over his waist, a chrome flash peeked out.

Tom questioned whether he should follow the young kid or move on him now. Another voice in his head grew louder. Time was of the essence. If he had any chance of saving Amanda, he couldn't wait.

By now, the Nova would be hot, so he needed to change vehicles. A Honda was as good a choice as any. Especially if it got him what he needed.

The soles of his tennis shoes touched the street. Jagged asphalt created potholes and cracks across the road. The county had long forgotten this neighborhood, and repairs neglected for at least a decade.

The sun baked the mixture of tar and oil, and the heat flowed up through his shoes. Tom ambled across the street as the Del Sol started and backed out of the driveway. The driver slid the little sports car right past Tom on the passenger's side. As the kid shifted from reverse, Tom grabbed the door handle, wrenched it open, and slid into the passenger's seat.

"What the fuck?" the kid shouted, reaching awkwardly for his gun.

Tom stretched his left hand across his body and caught the kid's wrist. With the flick of his wrist, he slammed the bony hand against the wheel. The chrome forty-five fell from the kid's hand. Tom's right hand shot forward, catching the pistol by the barrel as it bounced off the dash and tumbled to the floor.

"Shit!" the Latino kid howled, recoiling his hand.

"Calm down," Tom ordered as he shifted the forty-five around to hold the grip.

"What do you want?" the boy stammered.

"Drive," he demanded, leveling the barrel of the gun into the driver's gut. "I don't want to hurt you, but I will."

The kid nodded. "¿Dónde es?"

"Just drive," he repeated.

Nervously, the kid reached down and shifted into first gear. The car stuttered as he tried to move the knob to the second gear.

"I'm going to ask you some questions," Tom explained. "You are going to help me out."

The driver nodded again.

"Good," the man responded in a soothing tone.

The Del Sol approached an intersection, and the boy glanced over at Tom with unasked question.

"Left," he told him.

The car turned left after a rolling stop at the sign.

"Be sure to obey the law," Tom warned. "And use your blinker."

Another nervous head bob.

"What gang do you belong to?"

"Uh..." came the answer.

"No bullshit," Tom demanded. "What gang?"

"*Los Caballeros.*"

"The cowboys?" he questioned.

The kid shrugged.

"There's a local gang around here jacking cars," Tom told him. "Had a snake tattoo."

The driver's eyes cut toward him with some recognition.

"You know who they are?"

He responded, "Could be the *Serpientes.*"

"*Serpientes?*" Tom clarified.

Another shrug. "They are pretty bad."

"Bad how?" Tom asked.

"They run a lot of whores and drugs up from Central America. Guns too. I got that piece off a *Serpiente.*"

"And cars?"

"*No sé,*" he explained. "I don't know. Really."

"What about the Caballeros?" Tom demanded. "Where would they take a stolen car?"

The boy shook his head.

"The guy you got the gun from?" Tom asked. "Where is he?"

"I just got his number from a guy."

"What's the number?" Tom pressed.

"Hold on," the kid begged, sweating as he stared into Tom's cold eyes. "He called me last week."

He fumbled into his pocket, and Tom shoved the barrel of the forty-five into the boy's side, reminding him he was a squeeze of the trigger away from bleeding out in the car.

"Just my phone!" he exclaimed.

"Slowly," Tom urged, and the *Caballero* removed a red iPhone.

"Find the number." The fatherly Tom Harrod shroud withered with each second he bullied this teen. "If you try anything, I'll put one of these rounds through your liver. You'll be dead before I'm ten feet away."

The thug nodded in understanding. His face tightened, and Tom realized he never even considered calling for help. Once Tom planted the thought, the kid became even more aware of his situation. While he was behind the wheel, the *Caballero* knew he wasn't in control.

Were the roles reversed, things might be different. This kid lacked focus. He'd think the gun was enough to subdue him, and he'd grow lax. It was obvious—there'd be a moment when his attention would shift. That would be the moment to pounce. Slam the brakes and strike. If the opening was there, he would take the gun and shoot his captor. Or at the very least, use the butt of the chrome forty-five to batter the kid into unconsciousness.

But the roles weren't reversed, and this stupid gangbanger was on the verge of wetting himself.

Tom didn't care.

His eyes cut to the digital clock on the stereo.

One hour and seventeen minutes since he'd parked in front of the gas pump.

One hour and fifteen minutes since two *Serpientes* killed Audrey and Jackson.

He could feel the weight of the wedding ring in his pocket. The indention it was making in his thigh. His mind circled the inside where the words "Forever Mine" were engraved in the gold

One hour and fifteen minutes since the rules changed.

Since Tom Harrod died.

SEVEN

I jerked in surprise as a shrill blaring echoed through the Jeep. It took me a second to recognize it as the ringtone on my new phone. Most people adjust to the sudden interruption of thought their cell phones offer. This was technically my first cell phone since before I got out of the Corps.

It's not like I never used one. In the Corps, I carried one constantly. It was crucial to stay in contact with both my men and my superiors. I'd even borrowed one from the concierge at the Tilly Inn from time to time, but I didn't make it a habit to carry one. I certainly didn't expect to get calls on them. That was the number one reason I didn't have a mobile plan—I didn't want anyone calling me.

"Chase," I answered.

"Gordon," Scar growled.

"That was fast," I remarked.

He grunted in response. I'd found Scar wasn't a man of many words, and most of those were barely verbalized and only through clenched teeth.

"There's a guy over on 198th Street who handles a lot of cars. I doubt he's the only one, but on that side of the county, there aren't many."

"Thanks, Esteban."

"I have more," he offered bluntly, as if I'd grabbed just the Tootsie Roll from a bag of Snickers.

"I'm sorry," I told him. "What else?"

"*Las Serpientes,*" he commented like a sommelier presenting a merlot. "The snake on the arm is their brand. Probably unique designs, but that's likely who you are looking for."

"Who are they?" I asked.

"Motorcycle gang," Scar explained. "Or at least that's what they say. Not sure if a motorcycle is required to join or not."

"At least the rules aren't too strict," I remarked mirthfully.

"Hmm," he responded. "They came up from Guatemala. Not sure if they started there or here, but they are all *guatemaltecos*—Guatemalans."

I didn't ask, but wondered if there was a social dynamic between Cubans and Guatemalans, but it didn't seem important.

"Any chance you know where they hang out?" I asked instead.

"No," he answered curtly. "As I understand it, they have a couple of clubhouses, but they rotate between them. They aren't big, but they deal in some heavy shit, Gordon. Women. Guns."

"Drugs?" I questioned, wondering if they were competition for Julio Moreno or not. That might put them in Scar's crosshairs if his boss didn't like them treading on his turf.

"Most likely," he told me. I guessed it meant it wasn't a lot. Of course, it might be something he handled, eventually.

"Are they bringing it into the country?" I asked. It seemed unusual for gun runners and human traffickers to mix it up with carjackings, too. But I was far from an expert in virtually anything.

"From what I've been told, yes. My guess would be it's originating in Guatemala."

"They'd need a place to stash those kinds of things," I commented. Guns were easy—easily loaded in a container and dropped in the woods until someone bought them. Humans, on the other hand, were tricky. They needed food and water, but they also made noise.

"Hmm," he mused in what I guessed was agreement.

"The leader is named Xavier Jimenez. Don't know much about him. I'm sure I could find out what he ate for dinner yesterday if it was worth my time."

"Are you shaking me down?" I asked in jest.

"Hmm," he denied. It came down to what was worth it to Scar. Or rather, what was worth it to Julio Moreno? If I were a gambling man, I'd bet Scar went to Julio, who realized I was about to cross *Las Serpientes*. That told me enough about whether Moreno planned to do anything about their incursion into his territory. He'd give me all the information I needed—or at least that I thought I needed—to go after them. I might

have come to Scar and Moreno for a favor, but
they were smart enough to make it work for
them.

"Is the guy with the chop shop a *Serpiente*?"

"I doubt it," Scar stated. "He'll try to remain
unaffiliated to get more business."

"That seems risky," I noted.

"Risk versus reward," he explained. "But it will
catch up to him when he crosses the wrong
gang. Or more likely, he'll become too much of
a liability. Either way, he'll end up dead from
unnatural causes."

I stifled the chuckle, but remarked, "Are you
making a joke?"

Ignoring me, he said, "If you need anything
else, Gordon, call me."

Click. He was gone.

The offer at the end was out of character,
but it cemented the notion that Moreno was
pointing me toward *Las Serpientes*. I just hoped
I could trust Scar enough that this information
was valid. While he and I didn't see eye to eye, I
didn't think he'd steer me the wrong direction.

After finding the address Scar gave me on the
maps app the phone had, it took me twenty
minutes to find the shop on 198th Street. Five
of those minutes I spent trying to turn around
with a boat behind me.

I passed the address, driving slow. The gun-
metal finish on Jay's Jeep made it eye-catch-
ing, a trait one doesn't want when attempting
surveillance and reconnaissance. Add a twen-
ty-foot fishing boat, and the vehicle is more
than memorable.

It was nothing more than three buildings set in a V formation. The obvious garage appeared to be a former Texaco station, given the faded and worn circular sign with the red star. Texaco's logo had long since changed, but this one looked like it was from around thirty or forty years ago. Someone painted the roll-down garage door black, including the small windows. Chipped white paint and flaking concrete made up the rest of the building. A window that had once looked out over the gas pumps had several strips of tape across a crack stretching from one side to the other.

The other two buildings had more of a warehouse design. I could see one overhead garage door on the north side. The south side sported only a man door and a small dumpster with one panel rusted through. The trash flowing over the top indicated the container wasn't being serviced by any waste disposal companies. It might have been left over from the Texaco years, but I was shocked someone hadn't dragged it off as scrap metal. Perhaps whatever refuse was inside it made the quick salvage not quite so lucrative.

As I continued past, I found a spot on the street, three blocks away, that was long enough to accommodate the Jeep and Angler 204. When I got closer, I noticed two cars parked off to the north side. There was no sign of the old lady's Chevy Nova or Caleb. Or Thomas. Whatever he was going by. I had trouble wrapping my brain around the name Thomas Harrod. I recognized him as Caleb. Yeah, I didn't remember his last name, but "Caleb" must have imprinted on my brain.

Whoever he really was, I saw no sign of him.

It was still the middle of the afternoon, and there was no covert approach. I had to move unobtrusively, which meant don't look suspicious. I remember a sergeant who constantly referred to a line from one of the Star Wars movies. "Just fly casual," he'd warn.

Luckily for me, my daily attire didn't offer any warning signs. The shorts and tank top paired with a pair of Chacos might cause me to be mistaken for a beach bum—a notion that wasn't far from its mark. I preferred the term boat bum, but the distinction was sometimes gray. Either way, I hoped anyone inside the shop would only see an innocent passerby.

No one was outside the buildings. The only life I could see were the two cars parked on the north side next to the overhead door. Neither vehicle passed for inconspicuous, either. A newer Chevrolet Camaro convertible with a glittering gold finish all the way to its wheels, which I guessed was only a coat of gold alloy of some kind. A matte-black hood scoop rose above the engine. Besides the black cloth of the convertible top, the scoop was the only thing on the car that didn't reflect. Next to it was a late-eighties Impala with a turquoise paint job and custom wheels. The owner added lifts to raise the frame several inches. Both custom jobs probably cost more than my boat and most people's homes.

However, it was a flashing neon sign stating "Car Guys Are Here." Scar was correct—this guy would not survive long. If the local law enforcement wasn't already watching him, it wouldn't be long before someone noticed the nice street rides parked in front of a derelict building.

Survival in any form requires a level of preparation. Even criminals needed to consider that. The location appeared perfect for a chop shop. It was off the beaten path on 198th Street, and the buildings were the kind that could be boarded up and empty or simply storage for something else. If they'd keep it from looking occupied, they might skate past the police.

Not your problem, Gordon.

When I reached the south side of the buildings, I swept my eyes casually over the structure. No visible cameras. No open windows.

It would be foolish to assume there were no safeguards. Hidden cameras fit just about anywhere. I was fairly certain there were no sentries standing guard. Again, it seemed sloppy.

After I felt certain there were no eyes on me, I shifted my heading and slipped along the side of the building. The overflowing dumpster reeked of soured garbage. My lungs took in a deep breath of cleaner air before I inched around behind the rusting container. Thankfully, the heat dried up any puddles. I didn't think I had the courage enough to traipse through small cesspools in sandals. At least, I was glad I wasn't forced to find out.

A small window was on the wall about ten feet from the man door. The frame was only

twelve inches tall and set even with the top
of the door. No one bothered to paint over
it. Probably because of its height. My fingers
grabbed the ledge, and I pulled myself up. The
only thing I could see was the glint of the sun
gleaming off the dust covered glass.

A click followed by a creak startled me. I
dropped to the ground and scampered behind
the dumpster as the door opened.

Voices in Spanish. My pathetic high school
Spanish left me sorely unprepared for anything
that didn't involve ordering *cerveza* or *pollo*. I
didn't understand what they were saying, but
judging from the jovial tone and laughter, it
was just the kind of regular back and forth between guys. There were three distinct voices
yammering away. The rasp of a flint wheel in
a lighter sounded. The sudden aroma of cheap
cigarettes blended with the pungent air around
the dumpster. I couldn't tell if the cigarette
made it smell better or worse.

Three of them. The odds were not great for
me if they came around the corner. It was likely
I could outfight any of them, but it was a good
guess that at least one of them carried. I wasn't.
Of course, I had surprise on my side.

Better yet, just stay still. They won't walk
close enough to this dumpster to see me. Who
would? Just hunkering down beside it would
leave me with a serious scouring to get the lin-
gering scent of decay off me.

It seemed like a good plan.

Until the shrill tone erupted from my shorts.

Damn. Damn. Damn.

I fumbled to silence the phone, but it was too late.

"*¿Quién es?*"

I straightened up. Since surprise was no longer an option, I needed to get ready for whatever was about to happen.

"Sorry, guys," I offered, raising my hands apologetically. "I was just taking a leak."

The three men stared at me. The one with a cigarette hanging loosely from his lips narrowed his eyes at me.

"Who are you?" he questioned with a thick accent.

"Look, man," I explained, keeping my hands up as if in surrender. "I've been out and needed to pee, so I saw this dumpster. I figured who would care."

One of the others men had a half-inch ratchet protruding from his back pocket. He stepped toward me. "Why're you hiding?" he demanded.

"Like I said," I countered. "I didn't want to come out swinging. If you know what I mean."

The third one glanced at the other two and grinned, exposing a mouth missing at least three teeth I could count. It was the smile I'd seen on drill sergeants and bullies. Filled with anticipation of the reckoning it wanted to impart. I didn't like the simpering face.

These guys were amateur thugs. Lackeys whose job was to strip cars of whatever usable parts they could find. These guys took orders. They took shit, and here I was, a perfect receptacle for relieving the stress of their day.

Just because they were amateurs didn't change the numbers. So far, I'd seen no guns. I'd take my blessings however they came.

Gap-Tooth charged first. I knew it was going to be him. It was, after all, his idea, even if he never voiced it.

He lunged at me with a haymaker. His right fist swinging wide. Gap-Tooth was a powerful man—it was clear at first sight. If he clobbered me with that fist, he could knock me back into the wall. It's a forceful blow. But it's slow. The shoulder throws the fist out before the arm brings it back to its target. Even beginner boxers learn how to block a punch like that.

Me. I do more than block.

My left forearm popped up, parrying with his and deflecting his fist. He seemed surprised that his punch didn't land, and before he countered, I drove my right fist in an upper cut under his chin. The clunk as his bottom jaw slammed into the upper part of his mouth reverberated through my arm. My left arm, already cocked from the block, made it across to slam into this jaw. A tooth soared out of his mouth on a wave of saliva as he fell back.

From the corner of my eye, I saw the silver flash as the ratchet the second guy had in his pocket came slicing through the air at me. My right arm came up to shield my face, but the blow of a half-inch steel rod against my arm sent radiating shoots of pain up and down my arm.

"Arrr!" I roared, pushing the rage up at Ratchet's face with an open-palm jab. The bottom of my hand slammed into his nose, and my left hand whipped back to snatch the ratchet from his hand.

I was only moderately successful as I sent the tool skittering across the asphalt.

The cigarette-smoking one grabbed a two-foot piece of lumber with nails protruding from one side. His hands twisted up as he gripped it like a baseball bat. When he swung, I leapt back. My left hand cradled my right arm, which throbbed. I didn't think the bone broke, but it was nearly useless as it hung limply from the elbow.

Cigarette swiped at me again, and I dropped under the wood, and swept my feet out into his calves. My weight landed on my right arm, and the pain resonated through me, escaping in a howl of agony.

I rolled to my feet. Gap-Tooth was struggling to stand up, and I jumped up with a front kick that landed the ball of my foot into his nose. Ratchet tackled me, sending me slamming into the rusted dumpster. Debris fell off the towering pile onto us, and I drove my knee into his groin. Ratchet grunted and loosened his grip, instinctively reaching for his groin. As I twisted free, my left hand caught the back of his head, and I used the momentum of my spin to ram it into the dumpster.

I sucked in a breath as the man crumpled to the ground, lifeless. The impact on my back sent me forward, and nails raked through the tank top and dug into the skin on my back. I fell forward, catching the ground with my good arm as he swung at me again. As I rolled out of the way, I felt the ratchet I'd knocked free on my side. My right hand caught as Cigarette drove the lumber down on my shoulder. The sharp tacks stabbed into my skin, and when he pulled back the fabric of my shirt snagged the nails. I jerked away, pulling the board out of his grip. My weakened arm swung out, and the steel tool cracked into Cigarette's left kneecap.

Cigarette howled, and his knees buckled. My left hand grabbed the ratchet from my right, and I drove it with more force into the man's knee again. This time, the audible crack of bone offered me some satisfaction. He tumbled forward onto his good knee as I pulled myself up.

The dangling piece of lumber fell off my back, having pulled free of the threads of my shirt. I bent over and picked it up with my good arm. By now, the numbness and pain in my right arm subsided. Or maybe the rips across my back hurt more. Hard to say. Either way, I gripped the wood and swung like I was Hank Aaron standing at the mat with a tee ball waiting for a home run.

Cigarette fell over backward. He was lucky. I'd rotated the wood, so the nails didn't rip him up. His ribs broke, but at least he didn't have to worry about tetanus.

Gap-Tooth wasn't moving, but he was breathing. The same couldn't be said for Ratchet. A sliver of rusted metal stuck out from his eye. I cringed when I glanced down at him.

When I turned back to Cigarette, I heard him wheezing for mercy. I knelt down beside him.

"I'm looking for a Mercedes," I told him. "Help me out, and I'll walk away."

"We don't have one here," he wheezed, pushing away from me with his feet. Each movement caused his face to wince.

"What's come in today?" I demanded, stepping toward him. My back stung, and my arm throbbed now that the feeling was returning.

"Nothing," he muttered. "Nothing, I swear."

His eyes kept cutting over to Ratchet, who was now lying face up on the ground.

"Do you deal with *Las Serpientes*?" I questioned.

"Yeah," he answered. "Some."

"But nothing today?" I repeated.

Cigarette nodded vigorously.

"Where else would they go?" I asked.

"There's a guy north on 41. Guy named Ritchie up there works out of a storage place."

"Where?"

He gave me a general idea. The storage unit was on what Floridians have termed the Tamiami Trail on Highway 41. "He's just past the airboat guy," Cigarette explained.

I leaned forward and felt through his pocket to find his wallet. I removed his driver's license. Cigarette's face scowled in the little box in the corner. The ID listed his name as Lucas Fernandez. I tapped the card and smiled at him. "If you warn Carlos, I'll come back for you."

Cigarette stared up at me as I slipped the license into my pocket and walked away.

EIGHT

The acoustic ceiling tiles long yellowed were a clear sign that Carl Winston regularly ignored the No Smoking policy. The short, stout figure stared through wire-framed glasses at the screen in front of him. Numbers scrolled by as he made minor notes on a yellow sticky pad.

Stale air hung in the windowless unit. A fifty-inch television screen displayed a map of the Middle East with flashing symbols that resembled a high-tech strategic board game. Were it not for the screen hanging between two bookshelves, it might have been mistaken for any two-bit lawyer's office. The map was global, with highlighted dots and shaded countries.

He'd been in the chair for almost nine hours with only two five-minute breaks to sneak off to relieve his bladder. His morning began somewhere south of four in the morning, a time that required him to brew his own coffee. It only required him to flip the switch—Cassy prepped the coffee maker last night.

It was a dreaded season. Budget season. This time of the year was worse than dealing with most international crises. The Congressional Committee demanded more and more information before they'd finally allot the required funds to operate. Funding was a foregone conclusion, but these senators wanted to flex their muscles. Each request intended as a reminder to Winston that his office rested in the senators' grasp.

The whole pretense was utter bullshit. Winston knew it. The senators knew it. No one was going to vote against national security, and Winston's predecessor had packaged the Office of Compliance as the gatekeeper for intelligence. Winston operated as the Deputy Chief of Operational Security under the guise of Homeland Security. However, the activities of his office fell outside of the range the public knew.

Damned Krocker, he cursed to himself as he tried to find the figure Senator Jacob Krocker questioned yesterday during the committee meeting. The idiot was barely a sophomore Senator from Nebraska. He actually thought he was still campaigning in this classified, closed meeting. Still, he did, at least figuratively, control the purse strings. Maybe not the yes or no of the matter, but he could drag it out for weeks. Winston had far more important things to deal with over the next few weeks than jumping every time Krocker demanded it.

His stomach grumbled, and when Cassy came back, he'd get her to run find him a sandwich.

A knock at the door pulled him up from the rows of numbers.

Lee Hubbard, the senior analyst in his office, pushed the door open. Her nose instinctively crinkled at the musty office. Winston didn't let the housekeeping staff into his office, citing classified documents passed over his desk daily.

"Lee," Winston greeted. "What's up?"

Hubbard was in her early thirties. She'd scrambled up the ladder in the National Securities office and found a transfer to the Office of Compliance. The ginger hair was pulled back in a bun, hiding the long locks that normally hung down past her shoulders.

"A report just came across my desk directed toward you," she offered, somewhat demurely. Winston knew he intimidated her, which pleased him. Hubbard was talented, and the last thing he wanted was for her to shoe-horn herself into his job before he was ready. He had no intention of staying here forever, but he'd be damned if he let someone push him out.

"What is it?" he demanded, annoyed more at Senator Krocker still than Hubbard.

"A carjacking in Florida. Cops pulled some prints. They triggered an alert to this office for a file codenamed Corsair. Your name is attached to the file."

Winston straightened up in his chair. "Corsair?" He repeated the code. "Are you certain?"

Hubbard offered a shrug. "I can only go by the alert. These things can turn out to be nothing. Fingerprints cross-matched in the system. However, it seems like a solid match."

"Did you say a carjacking?" he questioned. His mind reeled. The numbers on the screen suddenly became unimportant.

"A family in South Florida was attacked at a convenience store. The thieves shot the mother and son. The father was inside the store when the shooting occurred. He was not injured."

"Who did the prints belong to?" Winston inquired.

"I believe the father."

Winston's left eyebrow arced. The father?

"How soon can you get down there?" he asked.

Hubbard pulled out her phone. It was just after three. "Let me see if I can get on a flight down there," she suggested. "A couple of hours if one is ready."

"Go, I'll call ahead," he assured her. "I promise there will be a plane ready to take off by the time you reach the airport."

Hubbard nodded. She wouldn't have time to pack, but she'd long grown accustomed to spur-of-the-moment excursions. A small duffel bag in her locker had two days' worth of clothes and toiletries. If she needed more, she'd find them in the field.

Most people found that lifestyle to be disconcerting, but Hubbard thrived on it. Too many weeks in the office wore on her. She wanted to be on the cusp of the action.

"Where's Vickers?" Winston asked her.

"Uh... I'm not sure," she admitted.

"Find him," Winston demanded. "I want him to meet you there if he's not in town."

She let out a sigh. Damon Vickers was less of an agent and more of a cleaner. He was the man Winston brought in to eliminate troublesome areas that infringed on the Office of Compliance. Hubbard was used to the vernacular, but it made it easier than saying Vickers came in to kill people who impeded the office and Winston in particular.

"Sir, can I ask what is Corsair?" she questioned, wondering what it was she was walking into if the main wet work agent was being brought in.

"Corsair is a who, not a what," he explained. There was no point in reminding Hubbard that what he was telling her was classified. Her clearance level was as high as Winston's. Well, almost as high. Winston guarded a few of his own secrets.

Hubbard stepped closer to the desk as Winston continued. "His name is Caleb Saunders, and he was likely the deadliest person to work in this office."

"He went rogue?" she asked.

"He ghosted," Winston answered. "Nine or ten years ago. I'll have to double-check the file. Corsair had a mission in Turkey, and he never came back."

"The mission?" she questioned, assuming the answer was a political target.

Winston shook his head. "He didn't accomplish it. We weren't sure what happened to him. Some figured him for KIA, but something about it nagged at me. I didn't think he'd die that easily."

Hubbard nodded. Winston was holding something back, but she expected that. She didn't trust him, never had.

"Why send Vickers then?" she asked.

"If Corsair was compromised, he'll need to be handled."

She stood motionless. There was no point in agreeing or disagreeing. However, if Corsair had been off the grid for nearly a decade, then he didn't seem like a compromised target. Nonetheless, she'd follow Winston's orders for now.

"Why would he resurface now?" she questioned.

Winston stared into the screen of numbers. His eyes glazed over as he thought. Finally, he asked, "How old was the kid who was shot?"

Hubbard shook her head. "The police haven't reported it."

"Do they have the father in custody?"

"No," she responded. "He stole a car and chased after the carjackers."

"They'll be dead then," he remarked, as if commenting on the ripeness of a pear.

"He's going after them?" Hubbard questioned, knowing it was only Winston's speculation.

"It seems safe to assume that Corsair found some domestic bliss after dropping off our grid. Someone just took that from him. I don't think he'll take too kindly to it. And no one is better suited to kill than Corsair."

"And if we get in the way?" she wondered.

Winston shrugged. "That's why you're taking Vickers. Corsair is a walking time bomb.
Not only is he deadly, but he has secrets that
shouldn't be floating around in public."

Hubbard sighed.

"Go," Winston barked. "Get on that damned
plane. I want the police report in my hands
three seconds after you get it."

Hubbard nodded, turning to leave.

NINE

G ravel crunched under the tires as Lonzo whipped the Mercedes-Benz GLC into the drive of the Complete Storage Needs. A motor on the automatic gate whirred as the gears turned, pulling the chain to open it. The chain-link jerked and bounced as it moved down the channel. Metal on metal screeched, and even inside the car, Lonzo winced as the pitch irritated his ears.

The Complete Storage Needs sat on two acres on the north side of Highway 41. An old gas station whose pumps had been gone since the late eighties operated as the office. Long white and orange metal buildings lined up parallel to the highway in five rows. Each row housed ten units with overhead garage doors.

A dark figure in the office waved, and all Lonzo could see was the silhouette of the person in the dirty window. The tires rolled forward as Lonzo steered slowly through the gate. Behind him, the screeching started again as the gate closed.

"It's to the right," Gaspar instructed. His tone had grown gruff since they discovered the girl in the car seat. He didn't want to bring her here, but Lonzo was insistent they couldn't kill her.

So far, she'd stopped crying. At least out loud. The tears might have dried up, but the constant sniffling and occasional gasp of air between sobs came from the back seat. Lonzo had a little sister. She was almost ten now, but he remembered when she was the same age as this girl. He knew he never was going to accomplish a lot in life. That much had been told to him since he was a child. His mother, who immigrated from the Guatemalan city of Quetzaltenango, berated him for everything he did wrong. She'd compare him to his father, a man he never knew because he left when Lonzo was six. No, he never expected to do well in school or make much out of himself, but he was a good *hermano*. He fought off older boys and threatened the younger ones when they gave Luissa trouble. This girl reminded him too much of his little sister. He couldn't stomach Gaspar's idea of throwing her into a marshy area to feed the alligators.

Besides, Lonzo thought, that would only tell the cops which way the two were heading. He didn't believe it was possible to hide the body forever. Someone would find her and connect the body to them.

"Over there," Gaspar pointed to the three open overhead doors.

Lonzo pulled up to the middle door. Someone had opened the three bays up to create a larger work area. They removed even the back wall to make it even deeper, taking up the three units on the opposite side of the building.

A head lifted over the opened hood of a silver Toyota Corolla. The Latino man was in his fifties with a graying beard covered with oil and grime. He studied the boys as they climbed out of the Mercedes.

"*¿Ustedes son Las Serpientes?*" he asked.

"*Sí,*" Gaspar responded, slamming the passenger's door. "Did Xavier call?"

"No," the man spat out in a derisive tone. "Xavier never calls."

The man strolled around the car.

"*¿Cuál es su nombre?*" Lonzo asked.

"Speak English, boy," the man scolded. "The name's Ritchie."

Ritchie opened the rear door and stared inside. His head cocked back and forth for several seconds, as if the child mesmerized him. Finally, he lifted his head to stare at Gaspar.

"What is this?" he demanded.

"He wouldn't let me kill her," Gaspar whined.

Ritchie turned his head back and forth between Gaspar and Lonzo. "Wouldn't let you kill her?" he repeated. "What the hell is wrong with you?"

"She's a witness," Gaspar pleaded in a voice that continued to gain a higher pitch.

"The girl is too young to remember anything," Lonzo argued. "There's no point in killing her."

"But you can bring her here?" Ritchie demanded. "That's the dumbest thing ever. You kidnapped her."

"We didn't know she was in the car," Gaspar whined.

"Did you kill the parents?" Ritchie asked. "I assume they were the ones driving."

"Killed the mom and her son," Gaspar boasted, his voice shifting down with pride.

"The dad was in the store," Lonzo pointed out.

Ritchie shook his head, pulled his phone out, and texted something.

"Who are you calling?" Gaspar shouted with insistence.

"Xavier," Ritchie answered. "I need to know what the fuck to do with you two."

Gaspar paced beside the car as Ritchie walked away.

"This is going to be bad," Gaspar cried. "It's your fault."

"Calm down, Gaspar," Lonzo urged.

"Don't talk to me like that," Gaspar snapped. "You're just a prospect. Barely that even. That tattoo don't mean shit. You got it yourself."

"Shut up boys," Ritchie demanded loudly. "Xavier is two minutes away."

"Dammit," Gaspar cried. He pulled his forty-five out and stormed toward the rear door.

"Gaspar!" Lonzo shouted, running around the car.

"Idiot!" Ritchie screamed. "Don't you dare do that."

"We need to get rid of her before Xavier shows up," Gaspar insisted.

"Not here, you don't," Ritchie corrected him. "I don't want no cops showing up looking for a dead girl. It's bad enough you brought her here. She damned well better be leaving here alive."

Gaspar stared at the older man. "What's Xavier going to say?" he asked.

Lonzo moved around toward the older *Serpiente*. "It's better if we ask him what he wants us to do?"

His head started shuddering. "He ain't going to like it."

Lonzo nodded. "But he'd like it less if we'd ruined the car. If we stopped to get rid of her, we might have gotten caught. Better to think it through now that it's happened."

Gaspar sighed with resignation.

"Put the piece up," Ritchie urged him. "No point in it going off on accident."

"We could sell her," Gaspar mentioned as he slipped the gun under his shirt.

"The girl?" Lonzo questioned.

Ritchie's right eyebrow twitched. "She's a little young," he remarked disapprovingly.

"She won't always be," Gaspar boasted. He seemed to like this idea better as he thought about it.

"I don't know," Lonzo interjected. "It might be better if we take her and just drop her off at a fire station. They let you do that with no problems."

"Right," Gaspar blurted. "There'd be cameras all over. 'Oh, look, we found a girl whose family was killed. I wonder who dropped her off. Oh look, it's those two idiots.'"

Ritchie shook his head. "None of this better be my problem," he explained. "No one gets killed here. All I do is get this ride ready to be sold."

The screeching of metal on metal echoed between the buildings, and Lonzo recognized the sound of the gate opening. A rumble weaved its way between the buildings ahead of the origin of the sound—a Harley Davidson Street Glide. A fiftyish Latino man with jet-black hair finely streaked with gray straddled the motorcycle. Dark aviator glasses shielded his eyes, and a thin leather jacket covered his shoulders and arms. The bike turned toward them.

The motorcycle's engine slowed, and the rider let his right leg down to catch the weight of the bike while his left pushed the kickstand down to catch it. When the engine died, the lack of noise was evident, as if the rumble of the 1900cc engine was expected to exist forever.

"*Mis hermanos,*" the man greeted them with a wide white grin. Without waiting for a reply, he swung his right leg over the saddle and straightened up.

The man stripped the leather jacket off like he was flaying himself, and Lonzo watched as the material stuck to his skin for a brief second. The jacket was solid protection should the rider fall off the bike, but once the ride was over, the Florida heat insisted he remove it. The leather jacket draped over the rear saddlebag.

He peeled the fingerless gloves off each hand, revealing the opening maw of a viper in mid-strike. The tattoo resembled Lonzo's except for the quality. Lonzo's was mediocre, done by a cheap local tattoo artist. The viper on the back of Xavier's hand was intricate and colorful. The artist created scales that appeared to have actual texture. Lonzo wanted to touch it, but knew better than to try or even ask.

Xavier walked past the two *Serpientes* without a word. The crunch of his boots on the gravel was the only sound. Lonzo realized he was holding his breath.

At the Mercedes, Xavier opened the back door and bent to look inside.

"Hello there," he greeted the girl.

Snuffling came from the car followed by a faint, cracked, "Hello."

"What is your name?" Xavier asked in a gentle tone.

"Amada," the girl responded.

"Amanda?" Xavier clarified.

Lonzo watched as the girl nodded her head.

"Okay, Amanda," Xavier told her. "I'm going to take care of something, and I'll take you home. Okay?"

She nodded again. "I want my mama," she said.

"I know, sweetie," Xavier responded, patting her head before shutting the back door.

"Xavier..." Gaspar began, but the man flung his right hand back, catching Gaspar in the face with a sold backhand.

He turned and threw his left in a fast jab that crunched against Gaspar's nose.

"What the fuck do you think you are doing?" Xavier demanded as he struck Gaspar again and again,

"I wanted to kill her," Gaspar pleaded, covering his face with his hands in defense. Instead of stopping, Xavier shifted his target to the man's torso, riddling his ribs with his fists.

"Lonzo wouldn't let me," he howled as his knees buckled.

Xavier stepped back and kicked the other man in the side. When Gaspar fell over, Xavier continued to drive the toe of his boot into the man's side.

Lonzo shirked back, scared to turn away and equally afraid he was going to be next. Or worse. Gaspar was a full member of *Las Serpientes*. At present, Lonzo was only a prospect. This was supposed to be his moment—his chance to be a patched member. Now he worried he'd just be a casualty. His eyes turned back to the girl in the back seat. Amanda. Gaspar was right. They should have taken care of her immediately.

"This wasn't Lonzo's doing," Xavier howled when he finally stopped hammering the man with his foot. "You were in charge of him. It was your job."

"*Lo siento*," Gaspar muttered, but it came out "*losito*."

"Apologies don't help me, Gaspar," Xavier announced.

"Yes, sir," Gaspar responded.

Xavier shook his head like a disappointed father. He bent over and grabbed Gaspar by the arm, pulling him up to his feet.

"This is a lesson, *hermano*," Xavier explained.

Gaspar nodded, but Lonzo didn't understand what the lesson was. He doubted Gaspar did, either.

"Go in the back and clean up," Xavier ordered. His demeanor had switched four times since he'd pulled up, and Lonzo didn't understand what to expect next.

Gaspar limped past Ritchie, whose sympathetic eyes followed the young man. The older mechanic followed Gaspar through another door.

Xavier turned to stare at Lonzo. He didn't move.

"I'm sorry, Xavier," Lonzo offered. "I didn't let him kill the girl."

"That's good," the leader told him.

Lonzo didn't respond. He was confused.

"It would have ruined the car," Xavier commented, repeating what Lonzo told Gaspar. "That would have been a waste of time and money. Not to mention a trail from the girl's family to us."

Lonzo nodded. "We didn't see her when we took the car," he explained. "I think she was asleep."

Xavier waved off his excuse as if it didn't matter. "Lonzo, what do we do with her?" he asked.

Lonzo's voice trembled. "Well, she's just a baby," he commented. "I don't think she could identify us."

Xavier's head tilted. "Depends on how long she stays with us," he remarked.

Lonzo agreed. "Gaspar suggested we sell her."

Xavier laughed. "Gaspar is an idiot, don't you think?"

Lonzo was too worried about answering that question. He continued, "He thought she'd grow up."

The leader shook his head slowly. "I'll take care of her," he promised the young man. "Now, tell me about the job."

Lonzo detailed everything that had happened until they drove away from the gas station.

"Were you seen?" Xavier asked.

"There were cameras, but we kept our faces covered. Gaspar warned me to stay out of the view."

Xavier offered an approving nod. "It's a good car," he beamed, staring at the Mercedes. "Good kill, too."

"Thank you," Lonzo muttered.

The older man's hand went into his back pocket, retrieving a stack of hundred-dollar bills. Ritchie appeared in the garage again.

"Give Gaspar his share," Xavier ordered. "He'll be in a piss-poor mood after this. You better be ready for him."

Lonzo took the stack of bills.

"Ritchie, when will you have this beauty ready for me?" Xavier asked the other man.

"Tomorrow afternoon," he assured Xavier.

"Do you have another car here?" Xavier questioned.

"There's the Charger," Ritchie answered. "It's in number five."

Lonzo looked at the leader. "What about the girl?"

"I'm going to take her with me," Xavier explained. "In fact, move her and the car seat to the Charger for me."

"Yes, sir," Lonzo answered.

The sound of Gaspar's retching echoed from behind the shop.

TEN

My arm screamed with every movement. Jay's Jeep was a manual, which meant I was moving my right arm a lot in order to keep it moving. At first, I didn't think the bone broke, now I wasn't sure. It certainly didn't break in two, but it wouldn't surprise me if there wasn't at least a fracture in the radius. Each shift of the gears sent shooting pains past my elbow into my shoulder.

Once I got back to the Jeep after leaving the chop shop, I wanted to get away from the scene as soon as possible. If Cigarette and his buddies had other friends, I might not be as lucky. And on the off chance Cigarette called the cops, the police might hold me up for a bit. I wasn't too worried about jail time—three against one is a clear-cut self-defense case. Most likely, they'd clean it up themselves. They didn't want police involvement.

No, I was more worried about the phone call Cigarette would make in the next few minutes. While he was going to walk with a limp for a bit, I didn't leave him incapacitated. The thought occurred to me, but I was far more hurt than I wanted him to realize. The debilitating blow to his kneecap was pure luck. With one arm barely functional, I needed to make a hasty retreat.

If he had a phone on him, he'd have used it within seconds of my walking away. If he didn't have a phone, he'd have to get inside to one. Either way, within the four minutes it took for me to hike back to the Jeep, he'd call someone. Once he made the call, it only mattered about the response time. I wanted to be gone before anyone showed up.

A crunch of metal on metal warned me to stop grinding the gears. Two blocks away, an El Camino with a glitter-green finish raced past me. Probably the response team Cigarette called in. I doubted they paid a lot of attention to a guy heading out with his fishing boat. It should make adequate camouflage.

The only downside was Cigarette told me where the other chop shop was. It was a safe bet I was en route there. I did, thanks to his driver's license, know who Cigarette was and where to find him. Hopefully, that threat was enough to warn him off.

My face winced as I used my right hand to fumble the phone out of my pocket. The little bastard caused my current predicament. I wondered who called me at that inopportune moment.

The missed call was from a Washington, D.C., number.

Shaw.

I hit the call back button and pinched the phone between my shoulder and head. My right hand rested on the gear shift, and I considered stopping somewhere for something to dull the pain.

On the other end, the phone rang twice.

"Shaw," the general answered. The husky tone of her voice immediately straightened my back.

"General, this is Chase Gordon."

"Lieutenant Gordon," she greeted. "Good to hear from you."

The way she said that would have made most people doubtful of her sincerity, but I actually heard the lilt of her voice change. For a woman who clawed her way up the ranks with men far inferior to her as a leader, a Marine, and a human, she allowed little inference in her voice. There would never be a question of what she meant when she spoke.

"I'm sorry to bother you, sir," I apologized.

"Not at all," she informed.me. "Are you all right? You sound strained."

My eyebrow lifted in surprise. Two sentences in our conversation, and she sensed something was wrong.

"Ended up on the wrong end of a tire iron. I'll carry on."

Shaw offered no more concern. "I doubt you called to just chat," she remarked.

"No, sir," I admitted. "I wanted to pick your brain."

"Indeed," she acknowledged.

"Earlier today there was a carjacking in Miami-Dade County. Jay Delp and I happened upon the scene after it happened. Two people were murdered—a boy and his mother."

"That seems tragic," Shaw noted.

"Yes, sir," I continued. "The father left in pursuit of the carjackers. Jay and I watched him on the surveillance video. We recognized him from Parris Island."

"He's a Marine?" Her interest piqued.

"When we were at Parris Island, his first name was Caleb. Neither of us can remember his last name. But he never finished training. At least with us."

"And your point, Lieutenant?"

"He is using a pseudonym—Thomas Harrod."

"And you want to know what happened to him?"

"Sir, if he was a Marine..."

"Then he still is one," she finished. "I'd have to look it up."

"I'm trying to get to him before something happens to him," I explained.

"Do you know where he's going?" she questioned.

"We think there's another child in the car the thieves took."

"Well, shit," Shaw muttered, dragging the "shit" out.

"Exactly, sir."

"You realize if he went AWOL, then he may be a wanted man," Shaw suggested.

"I think he knew he was about to be hunted. There was something I saw in his eyes on the surveillance video. I've seen that look before."

"No doubt," she stated. "I'll see what I can find out for you. If I can share it with you, I will."

"Thank you, sir."

"Lieutenant," Shaw added.

"Yes, sir."

"Even if he isn't a Marine," she started.

"Sir, I don't care for people who kill mothers and their children."

"No, you don't, do you?" she replied. "I'll call you back."

The phone clicked off, and I let it drop off my shoulder onto the console between the front seats.

The chop shop Cigarette told me about was at least an hour away. A little longer since I was still dragging a boat along behind me. I needed to call Jay, but I didn't want to move my hand off the gear shift yet. The pain was currently at a throbbing six instead of the nine or ten I felt when I shifted gears. Might as well let it rest while I was cruising the highway.

Highway 41 begins in Miami. If one wanted to get technical, it begins at the intersection of Brickell Avenue and Carlos Arboleya Boulevard. To continue east on the street that turns in to 41 would only take one across the causeway to Brickell Key, a small man-made island just off the Miami River. But the highway doesn't stretch that far—probably an intentional ploy to keep the residents of Brickell happy. Instead, it stretches from Brickell Avenue across the bottom tip of Florida. Once 41 is out of the urban sprawl of Miami and crosses Florida 997, everything south of it is Everglades or Keys, mostly.

It's a gorgeous stretch of road lined with canals that, during the dry season, are also lined with alligators. Occasionally, like today, one of those beasts crossed the road. Sometimes, like today, the bastards take their sweet time.

A small line of cars stacked up behind me as this eight-foot alligator moseyed over the asphalt. The hot blacktop didn't seem to faze him, and he actually stopped for several seconds. Traffic heading east piled up too. I counted twelve cars heading toward Miami. In my rearview mirror, I could see six vehicles. All for a reptile. Had it been a turtle, I'd be quick to jump out and assist with its crossing. Much like most of life, there was nothing to do but wait for this fellow to pass on his own.

After fifteen minutes, I began to think the gator was taking its time on purpose—showing us humans who was boss. After all, there were very few opportunities for him to exert himself like that.

The ripped skin on my back burned. I couldn't remember when I had my last tetanus shot. Probably while I was still in the Corps. Of course, I'd seen the inside of a hospital once or twice since then, so it was possible.

At least I was feeling my back now. The pain in my arm had been occupying most of my parietal lobe. As the throbbing dulled somewhat, the stinging on my back became noticeable. I wish I could say this was a blessing, but the truth was everything hurt.

Finally, the alligator slipped off the road and onto the slope. His tail swept along behind him as he vanished into the brush. I didn't wait around to see him slide into the water. It's still fascinating, but I wanted to reach the chop shop before anyone else did.

What I would say if I found Caleb there still eluded me. I couldn't blame him, and if I were in his position, there's no chance a long-lost face would stop me. Perhaps I could facilitate his escape. Or would he even need to escape? He was trying to rescue a kidnapped child.

The shop Cigarette described was in the back of a self-storage unit. I pulled up the satellite image provided so readily by Google. The plot of land was narrow, with four or five hundred feet of road frontage. On the back side of the property, a thin canal which fed into a bigger swamp.

Cigarette did not know what the layout was. He swore he'd never actually been there. He was lying, but I didn't take the time to force the truth out of him.

As I pulled up to the storage place, I braked suddenly. Underneath the sign reading, "Complete Storage Needs," the automatic gate was wide open. Slowly, I pulled the Jeep through the opening. The chain-link gate clicked back and forth as if caught in a cycle.

Past the fence, what looked like an old filling station someone converted into the office. A red Honda Del Sol from the mid-nineties sat between the poles where the gas pumps would have been twenty years ago.

I could tell by the sign on the door that read "Office." Nothing gets by me.

Not even the figure slumped over the desk in the window.

Eleven

Blue-green water stretched across Doha Bay. The last bits of sun glittered on the chop. A large white yacht, trying to get into port before dark, motored into the bay. Only one floor below the glass dome atop the Burj Doha, Mahmoud Abbas waited as the demure woman poured a cup of Karak tea. Chocolate-colored liquid filled the empty cup. The woman held her gaze on the floor as Mahmoud took a sip. The pot had cooled since she brought it to his office an hour ago. When she attempted to take it away to refresh it with hot tea, he waved her off. This was his last cup before he dressed for dinner. Besides, while he didn't voice it, he preferred the tea a little above room temperature.

When the woman left without a sound, he rotated the chair around to stare out the wall of glass, looking down from the forty-sixth floor. The yacht in the harbor resembled a toy floating in a bathtub. His office faced south, but the 180-degree view allowed him to swivel to watch the night sky encroaching on Doha.

The cinnamon flavor melted over his palate. These last few minutes of daylight were a respite for the man. It was the signal his day was over—at least his day behind the desk. Abbas never ceased working. Dinner tonight was with Halim Nassim, a delegate of the Hausa tribe. The increasing violence in Sudan prompted tribal leaders to seek better armaments.

Thanks to the United States of America, there was an endless supply coming out of Afghanistan right now. Abbas needed only to broker the deal with Nassim. Normally, he'd have sent Khalim or one of his underlings to meet with Nassim. However, this meeting came at the request of Amir Tayeb, the chief of the tribe. Abbas planned for this evening to birth a new partnership with the Hausa tribe, one where Abbas supplied Tayeb with tanks and missiles enough to establish a strong foothold in their country.

Of course, he planned to send his own emissary to the opposing tribes. Ongoing tribal conflicts were far more profitable than seeing one side climb atop the others victorious.

A click behind him startled Abbas, who turned enraged that his brief reprieve was interrupted. Salar Tolzar, Abbas's head of security, stepped through the double mahogany doors. His Louis Vuitton loafers clicked across the marble floor.

Abbas stared at the man with growing concern. Tolzar wasn't a man to violate Abbas's space unless it involved matters of utmost import. Abbas employed Tolzar almost two decades earlier. The young man had been enlisted with the Kuwait National Guard when an

explosion left him with only nine fingers and a
scorched face. Tolzar covered the defect in his
hands with black gloves equipped with a pros-
thetic finger. The scarring on his right cheek
provided a permanent reminder of that fateful
day. A mutual acquaintance suggested Tolzar to
Abbas, who employed him under his previous
head of security. Tolzar proved himself to be a
loyal and efficient asset.

"Sir," the security chief announced in Arabic.
"My apologies for interrupting you."

"What is it?" Abbas questioned.

"I've received a report."

Abbas studied the man as he leaned back in
his chair. He rested the tea cup gently on the
saucer before folding his arms to give Tolzar his
full attention.

"Corsair has surfaced."

Abbas straightened in his chair quickly,
brushing his elbow against the tea cup and
splashing Karak tea over the wooden desk.

"Corsair?" he questioned with fiery eyes.
"Where?"

"In the United States," Tolzar explained.
"Florida."

Abbas placed both of his thick hands on the
top of the desk and pushed himself slowly to
his feet. His eyes stared through Tolzar. Finally,
he stepped in a semi-circle around his chair
to the expansive window. By now, night had
fully overtaken the bay, and the lights inside
the office reflected the white walls against the
window, obstructing any view Abbas had.

From the waterfront, Doha Tower would light up like a rocket. The towering spire at its peak pointed toward the stars, and the cylindrical phallic building would have been the crowning jewel in most cities. In Doha, it wasn't in the top five.

The lone figure standing in the window on the forty-sixth floor was motionless.

"Corsair," he finally whispered to himself.

"Yes, sir," Tolzar confirmed. "I reached out to a contact in the Office of Compliance. It hasn't been confirmed, but they lifted his fingerprints from a crime scene."

"Who do we have in the States?" Abbas questioned.

"I don't know, sir," Tolzar admitted. "I can have a list in just a few minutes."

"Never mind that," Abbas exclaimed. "Find someone and get them there immediately."

"Yes, sir," Tolzar acknowledged.

"I'll offer a hefty fee if they deliver Corsair to this penthouse. I want to remove the man's head with my blade." His gaze shifted along the reflection in the mirror until he stared at the sword hanging above the fireplace.

The blade was a gift from his son. The last gift from Farid. It was a token to Farid Abbas from Sing Chon, one of Kim Jong-Il's generals in 2008. Farid offered it to Abbas after the deal was struck. It was the last time he saw Farid.

Mahmoud Abbas reflected on the last day of Farid's life. He'd set up a rendezvous with Chon's people on a small atoll off Taiwan to make the trade. The remote location should have provided enough security, but somehow the man he later learned was called Corsair infiltrated the area. Both Chon's and Farid's contingents were small, but Corsair boarded the freighter where the two men were meeting. When Corsair disembarked, his son and Sing Chon were both dead. The United States government swept in to confiscate the weapons and freighter. No doubt those same arms were sold by the CIA under another guise.

Abbas spared no expense to track down his son's killer. It took years to scrape even a codename off a former CIA agent. After that, he heard Corsair was off-grid, either killed in action or in hiding. His contacts believed he'd been killed on a mission. Despite his best efforts, Abbas never discovered the details of Corsair's last mission.

Corsair developed into a legend, and Abbas crossed paths with others who saw the assassin's handiwork. Most described him as efficient and thorough. Others found him merciless and unstoppable. Whispers of his killing children and women perpetrated the myth. Almost every one of those people wanted to hire him for their work.

Not Abbas. He vowed to hunt the man down and kill Corsair himself. Over time, he'd fantasized about beheading the American. It grew into an obsession, and when word of Corsair's demise found him, Abbas sank into his grief again. There seemed to be no hope of avenging his son. It wasn't enough for Corsair to be dead—Abbas longed to see the man's eyes before he killed the Corsair. The killer needed to know why he was dying.

Now, nine years after he'd heard the man was likely dead, hope peaked out of the ground like the first sprout of grass through the snow. The obsession returned, flaming through Abbas's world as if it were a falling star. His attention pulled to the shining beacon.

"Salar," he called. "Put out the word everywhere. I'll pay twenty million pounds to the man who brings him to me alive."

"Alive?" Tolazar repeated.

Abbas smiled. "I said nothing about unharmed. Only alive and aware."

"Yes, sir," the security chief responded. "If that's all?"

Abbas continued to stare at the reflection in the room. He offered a single nod, and Tolazar excused himself with a slight bow.

As the muscled security chief exited the room, he regretted informing Abbas of his discovery. Tolazar was only working under Halid, Tolazar's predecessor, when Farid Abbas died. He'd seen the ripple effects surrounding the man's death. His father, enraged with grief, demanded this Corsair's head. Only at the time, Corsair was only a ghost. Halid failed at every turn to discover the man's identity, and before long, he fell out of favor with Abbas.

While his mentor fell, Tolazar found a way to excel. It was Tolazar who contacted an old CIA operative he'd known from Kuwait. The man, now several years closer to retirement, had a penchant for opium and young ladies. Once the agent returned to Washington, he wanted his forays in the desert to stay over here. Tolazar impressed upon the man his appreciation in the matter, and within a week, he had the codename, Corsair.

But despite the inner contact, Corsair amounted to nothing but a name. Even that, Tolazar wondered, might not have been true.

In 2016, Tolazar discovered a shadow agency called the Office of Compliance. While no evidence existed, he and a few others in his field believed this agency controlled Corsair and possibly more assassins. However, word from those in the know said Corsair was dead.

If today's news garnered nothing new, Tolazar worried his boss would become entrenched in his obsession again—to the detriment of all.

TWELVE

After my encounter with the Three Stooges earlier, I learned my lesson. I had no intention of trying to go in unarmed. Unfortunately, I planned to be on a peaceful fishing trip. My M45 handgun remained tucked away in the secret compartment in my berth aboard *Carina*. I opened the console on the Jeep. Jay Delp was nearly as reliable as I expected. Underneath a stack of fast-food napkins, I found a Heckler & Koch forty-five with two extra magazines.

If I'd dug around in the back seat, it wouldn't have surprised me to find at least two more guns stashed. Of course, Jay was a cop, meaning he considered himself always on duty. I'm just a bartender, occasionally. I suppose I should keep a bottle of vodka in my car—if I had a car.

The pistol's grip fit into my right hand. The muscles still refused to cooperate with me, and I struggled to hold it until my arm finally seemed to agree to work. After I pulled back the slide with my left hand to ensure the first round settled in the chamber, I climbed out of the Jeep. Thin brown streaks stained the driver's seat, and I already heard Jay's voice in my head, barking at me about bleeding all over his seat.

The Jeep remained between me and the office. I wanted to keep it that way for a few seconds until I knew no one tried charging out. Or worse—shooting.

The rest of the yard seemed relatively quiet. The H&K hung at my leg, inconspicuous to drivers racing by on the highway. If I'd held the barrel aloft like they do in those action books, every passerby would phone the cops about it. Discretion is always the smarter.

After several seconds, I ventured around the hood of the Jeep and jogged toward the red Honda. So far, no one shot at me. I counted that as a success so far.

The gun still hung at my side. Even if I tried to lift it up, I wasn't sure my arm would hold it for long. If I needed to shoot, I'd end up needing to swap hands, but if someone watched me, they might not notice the flaccid arm dangling. They'd just see the gun—I hoped.

The office door was closed, but I pushed it open gently with my right foot. The figure at the desk held a thirty-two-caliber pistol. A cell phone lay on the desk as if it fell out of his hand. The headrest of the office chair he sat was smeared with globs of blood and brains. A drawer on his right hung open. From the angle of the shot, the shooter stood about where I was.

If I were to guess, the man in the chair reached for the thirty-two in the drawer. His killer didn't let him get it much out of the drawer before he shot him. The bullet blew through the guy's skull, snapping the head back against the chair before he bounced forward. If I lifted this head, I'd likely find a nice clean hole somewhere in the middle of his face. Right between the eyes.

Most people might think that's a tough shot. It depends. At three feet, anyone with a modicum of accuracy could do it. The problem is the actual doing. It's one thing to shoot a guy from twenty to thirty yards away. Even to shoot someone in the back. But to stare into someone's face when they put a bullet with such precision between the very eyes looking back at the shooter takes a strong stomach. Or an intense hatred.

Careful not to touch anything, I stepped around the desk. Blood splatter on the floor had dried, but I crept around the droplets as if it was a minefield. My toes pushed the door behind the desk open, revealing a small studio apartment. Six hundred square feet, I estimated. A rumpled, full-size bed faced an orange and brown love seat with chunks of faded mustard-colored foam poking through the torn fabric. Stains that I hoped were only coffee covered the seat cushions in Rorschach-like splotches. A thirty-two-inch flat-screen television sat on a 1960s-era table with spindled legs curving in bulbous shapes.

There was nothing here. I maneuvered around the blood splatters again and stepped back outside.

Should I close the gate? I didn't want an innocent customer showing up to find Grandma's
silver set and stumble across the corpse in the
office. I needed to call Jay, but I wanted to make
sure Caleb wasn't here.

No. Closing the gate would take too long. I did
not know where to find the controls.

Instead, I moved around the building. The
storage units stretched out on either side of a
driveway. I didn't count the units in the white
and orange buildings, but it seemed like the
owners packed a lot of storage space on this
small plot of land. Worn ruts ran down the
gravel drive that bisected the middle, a result
of heavy traffic.

The H&K remained at my side as I walked
along the edge of the drive. On either side of
the road, the storage units appeared empty. No
one fired a shot at me. Again, this was still a
good thing.

As I stepped around the second building,
I froze. My right arm came up, quivering
as the weight of the H&K tried to drag it
back down. Three overhead doors gaped wide
open. Parked in the middle bay, a black Mercedes-Benz GLC sat with its hood raised. The
driver's door hung ajar. Stretched out beside it
lay the body of a man in mechanic's coveralls.

I crossed the clearing, putting my back to the
wall next to the open bay on the right. A radio
played a loud Latina woman singing something
fast and upbeat, but unfortunately for me, in
Spanish.

After inhaling a deep breath, I stepped around the corner, keeping the gun at the ready. The music echoed off the metal walls with the tinny ringing of the songstress's high-pitched notes. Nothing moved in the bays.

Whoever set up the garage had demoed the walls, separating six different units. On the back wall, another open overhead door allowed the sunlight to spill onto the concrete floor. From where I stood, I saw past the drive that bordered the lot and into the glades behind it.

I walked next to the Mercedes. Next to the mechanic was a nine-millimeter and a small electric screwdriver. He'd been removing the dash of the Mercedes, judging from the pile of screws and loose dash. I peered through the windshield, staring at the gap he'd created behind the dash. Were they smuggling something? Was that behind all this? It was possible Caleb moved drugs. The family on vacation made for a good cover story. Any cop that would stop them would see the kids in the back seat and pass them off as innocent.

That didn't track with what I saw on the video. Not that anything I saw offered more than my conjecture, but I trusted my instincts. The man on the video wasn't smuggling drugs.

That didn't mean someone else didn't do it for him—or to him, rather. Stash the drugs in a car and let the family unwittingly drive it where it needs to go. Then just grab it with whatever means necessary.

Wouldn't work. Too many variables. Kids get tired or sick. Too difficult to have a timetable set in stone.

No, this was still random. There was no point in trying to knit it into something that didn't fit.

I walked around the front of the Mercedes. On the back wall, there was a drill press—the kind used to bore holes in auto parts. I've seen them before in garages. Usually, the bit is stainless steel or even a diamond-edged bit for cutting through the thicker steel. I couldn't identify what kind of bit was on this press. The metal spiral punctured through the temple of a young Latino boy who hung from the drill press like soiled laundry.

I swallowed hard. Bloodied holes riddled the boy's arm where the press had punched through the skin, muscle, and bone. Blood crusted over his forearms and hands, but not enough to hide the snake tattoo coiled down his forearm. The snake's head, tattooed on the boy's hand, had two holes drilled through the eyes of the viper.

Caleb beat me here. He tortured the kid, probably after recognizing him as the one who shot his son.

If the kid was twenty, it would shock me. His whole life had been ahead of him. But it wasn't Caleb that ended that for him. He pulled that trigger. The kid might as well have shot himself. I didn't feel sorry for him.

I wondered how long ago this had happened. The blood had already dried, but that didn't take long. I might have gotten here in time to find Caleb if I hadn't waited on an alligator. Or he could have been here an hour ago while I duked it out with Cigarette and the boys. It didn't matter—I was too late.

If the kid with the snake tattoo knew anything, Caleb got it out of him.

A box of nitrile gloves sat on the edge of the counter next to the radio, playing a more soulful Spanish song from a baritone. I still didn't know what they sang. Donning a pair of gloves, I felt along the kid's pockets for a phone. My search was careful to avoid contaminating the body. When I found nothing, I walked over to the mechanic and searched his pockets, too. I pulled an iPhone out of his pocket.

Despite being dead, his phone opened up with the facial recognition software. It took me a second to scroll through the messages. My finger paused when I recognized a name—Xavier.

Scar told me the leader of *Las Serpientes* was a man named Xavier. The messages were in Spanish. The last one, stamped an hour and nine minutes ago, read, *"Tus chicos aparecieron con el Mercedes. Tienes un problema. Tienen una niña."*

My tenth grade Spanish never progressed much past the first semester. It certainly didn't improve in the eleventh grade when Coach Walker taught it. He let us watch *We Are Marshall* dubbed over into Spanish. Three times in one year. I hated that movie in English—I certainly didn't watch it in Spanish.

Despite that, I had picked up a few words. *Niña* meant "girl." Since Mercedes was self-explanatory, and *problema* sounds a lot like "problem," I figured the guy messaged Xavier that they brought a girl in with the car. At least, that's what I hoped. It might mean the missing kid was still alive. At least an hour ago. It also told me the Harrod child was a girl—something I needed to share with Jay.

Actually, I needed to share all of this with him. With three bodies, Caleb was racking up a hefty count. If I didn't loop Jay in, he couldn't decide how to direct the investigation. Jay tended to go out on a limb, and while I didn't mind scooting to the end, I needed to protect his reputation.

As I pulled the phone out of my pocket, something rattled behind the building. With some strain, I lifted the H&K and moved toward the back door.

Could be an alligator that slipped up from the water. Or it might be the kid. Somehow, I didn't think either was accurate.

I stepped out of the overhead door. The drive behind the building was only twelve feet wide, with a two-foot grass barrier between it and the slope toward the canal. Several fifty-five-gallon metal drums lined the back wall, stacked in a small pyramid. The one closest to the door had a funnel jutting from the opening. Used motor oil dripped down the funnel. Worn tracks cut through the grass and down the slope. The scarred ground almost perfectly matched the two-wheeled dolly under the oil drum.

Why bother paying to dispose of old oil when they can haul it out into the swamp and dump for free? Personally, I thought of plenty of reasons not to do it, but I suppose a group that has no problem gunning down innocent mothers and children doesn't squabble too much with the morality of polluting a natural resource.

A cough behind me caused me to snap around in a spin, leveling the gun at a kid sprawled on the ground. The boy's face had been bloodied and bruised. His nose twisted to the right in an unnatural direction. He stared at me with his arms holding his chest. A wheeze escaped his chest as he took a breath. On his right arm, I spotted a snake tattooed around his forearm.

He lifted his arms slowly above his head in surrender.

The second shooter? The one who shot the mother?

THIRTEEN

L ee Hubbard had never had much doubt that Carl Winston had some pull. Still, it had been just over two and a half hours ago that he sent her out of his office after this Corsair lead. By the time she reached the airport, only a few miles from the office building which housed the Office of Compliance, he'd not only arranged a Gulfstream, but the jet waited, fueled and ready to take off.

The man she only identified as Vickers was already on the plane. He sat with his back to her and his eyes closed. The six-foot-four man crossed his hands across his waist. White hair spiked up on his head, streaked with swaths of jet black. If she hadn't taken a second glance, Hubbard might have thought he'd intentionally dyed it. There was enough inconsistency in the striations for most to dismiss the concept.

Vickers had been Winston's go-to guy for jobs that required a certain lack of ethical confliction. If one of the Congressional Oversight Committee members asked if the Office of Compliance perpetrated any assassinations, Winston had no qualms about answering negatively. Vickers wasn't an official agent of the Office of Compliance. At least not as far as Hubbard could find. She'd never admit to digging into the man for fear it would only put a target on her.

Carl Winston had as little trouble tasking an assassin to this job as he did arranging the last-minute flight.

Vickers didn't speak during the entire flight. In fact, Hubbard never saw his eyes flinch. He sat motionless for just over two hours. His eyes appeared closed, but she thought perhaps he left a slit open to watch her. Even as the plane landed, the man didn't move.

She tried to ignore him. Instead, she dug through the file she had on Corsair.

Caleb Saunders.

There was very little about his life before he'd become embroiled with Carl Winston. He was born in Northeast Georgia and raised just south of the North Carolina border in the town of Clayton. His parents died in a plane crash when he was three years old. After that, his grandfather raised him. When Saunders was seventeen, a major coronary killed his guardian. Two months later, the boy graduated from high school with a four-point grade point average and the award for the USA Today Offensive Player of the Year. He had been a running back for his school's football team, and he was the only player ever to win the award that didn't eventually play in college or professionally. He simply never played again.

There were some articles about him in the Clayton Tribune after he led Rabun County High to win the State and then National Championships. He posed in a photograph with his grandfather, Phillip Saunders. The boy was in his football uniform with sweaty hair matted to his forehead.

The file said that Saunders graduated from high school and skipped college, despite the many scholarships offered. Instead, he drove himself the day after graduation to the United States Marine Corps Recruitment Office in Eastanollee, Georgia, and signed up with the Marines.

Hubbard continued reading. Based on his records, he never completed basic training. His paperwork bore the stamp, "Discharged." There was no reason attached, and no one noted the discharge as either dishonorable or honorable. Just "Discharged."

There was no record of his being recruited into the Office of Compliance. In fact, if Winston hadn't told her that Caleb Saunders was Corsair, she might not have connected them. The Corsair file carried Saunders's fingerprints, which was how the system flagged the report. However, nothing else noted the identity of Corsair.

She didn't believe there was no evidence. Winston was a smart man. He'd purged the connection. There was no need to wonder why he'd let her learn the details. By involving her, he was making her complicit. She understood he was using her, but that didn't stop her. Hubbard had plans, and crossing Winston would not help her. Better to play the game, letting him think she was unaware of his machinations.

When the plane finally came to rest, Vickers opened his eyes and stood up. He retrieved a case from the forward compartment and exited the plane without a word. Hubbard shook her head, gathered her files and bag to follow him.

A black Lincoln sat just off the runway. Arranged by Winston, Hubbard assumed.

She found Vickers in the passenger's seat, leaving her to drive. She bit her lip and placed her bag in the trunk. When she got behind the wheel, she turned to stare at Vickers.

"Since you're with me now, do you want to discuss what we are doing?" she asked.

"No," he replied.

Hubbard felt the blood in her cheeks press against the skin. "No?" she repeated.

"No."

"That's not going to work for me," she snapped. "I'm the lead on this."

Vickers didn't respond.

"Do you know who we are after?" she questioned, her voice nearly huffing as she spoke.

"Caleb Saunders, code-named Corsair," Vickers replied. "Former agent who went dark ten years ago. Confirmed kills—sixty-two. Suspected kills—twenty-three. Possibly living under the alias Thomas Harrod."

She glared at him.

"Would you like to discuss his training record?" Vickers asked coldly.

"Fuck you," she mumbled as she started the car.

In fifteen minutes, the black Lincoln bounced between two Miami-Dade Police Department patrol cars. A officer waved for them to stop, and Hubbard ignored him until the four tires of the Lincoln cleared the curb.

"You can't park here," the officer ordered as Hubbard stepped out of the car. "Ma'am, I said, you can't park here."

Hubbard flashed her identification with the Homeland Security seal on it. "Homeland Security," she blurted out. "Who's in charge here?"

"Ma'am, you can't park here," he repeated for the third time.

Hubbard turned her head slowly, locking eyes with the officer. He was barely a man, she noted. Barely twenty-five, if that. His smooth face had soft skin. He was cute, like one of those baby animal videos. Relegated to keeping people away from the scene—he was a rookie. So when she glared at him, the man's pupils dilated as he stared back at her. His right hand lifted, pointing to a chunky man in his late forties.

The portly man wore round glasses. He stood hunched slightly. Arms crossed over the round paunch, pressing through the short-sleeved shirt. His whole body fidgeted the way an addict does when the first cravings appear. The man shifted from his left to his right foot over and over. Beside him stood a tall, thin man at least ten years younger. That one looked like he was about to go camping. He wore one of those rust-brown fishing shirts with loose jeans and waterproof boots. Attractive, Hubbard thought. Almost like Tom Selleck without the mustache. He carried a confidence about him, but he was deferring to the older cop.

Hubbard turned to Vickers. "Wait here."

His upper lip curled, which she took for the equivalent of a shrug. There was no one to kill here, so he was happy to let her be in charge. At some point, she realized, his attitude would change. Hubbard needed to be ready for that. If she was going to maintain control, she wanted a plan. Because Vickers was a gigantic unknown variable. She could tell him all day who was in charge, but the man only had one leash. It belonged to Winston.

That was a problem for another time. For now, she took long strides toward the two men. Her skin felt the Florida air as if it was crawling across her. It wasn't sweat, but almost like she'd just walked through a mist filled with syrup.

The younger one saw her coming. His reaction was odd. She'd dropped into crime scenes on more than a few occasions. Most of the time, her appearance annoyed the local law enforcement. They had a tendency not to hide it. This guy remained nonplussed. A second later, the older one caught sight of her and visibly sighed. That was something she recognized.

"Fed?" the older asked when she was within a few feet.

"Lee Hubbard, Homeland Security." She showed him the same ID she'd flashed the officer.

"Homeland," the younger one repeated with a heavy drawl.

"Steve Arwoods," the older one introduced himself, extending a hand. "Chief of Detectives for Miami-Dade Police Department."

Hubbard shook the detective's hand, gripping it firmly. Her eyes turned toward the second man.

"Sorry," he apologized. "Jay Delp."

"Are you a detective too?" she asked.

"Yes, ma'am," he responded. She couldn't place what state he was from. Alabama? Mississippi? "Just not with Miami-Dade?"

Hubbard cocked her head curiously.

"Chief Delp is with Palm Beach County," Arwoods explained. Before she could ask the next question, Arwoods stated, "He was the first person on the scene after the murders."

Delp folded his arms with a certain satisfaction that Hubbard liked. "Agent... Is it agent?"

She nodded.

"Agent Hubbard," Delp continued. "What is it that brings Homeland Security to a carjacking?"

Hubbard glanced at Arwoods as if to ask why an outsider was questioning her. He responded, "I'm curious too."

She felt the sigh, but forced it back. "You triggered a national security alert," she answered.

"National security?" Delp questioned with this Gomer Pyle tone. "It looked like a gang initiation or something."

"I'll need to decide that myself," Hubbard advised. She suspected that Jay Delp knew plenty more than he let on. It was almost as if he expected her to show up.

"What can we do for you?" Arwoods asked.

"The husband," she explained. "I'd like to talk to him."

Arwoods made a halfhearted shrug as if it was out of his control, saying, "He's not here. We suspect he chased after the killers in another vehicle."

"Do we know which way?" she asked, looking directly at Delp.

Delp offered a smile as he pointed south on the road. "Video showed him pulling out and heading that direction. There are plenty of places he could have turned. Or he might have just kept driving into the Keys."

"Why would he do that?" she asked.

"I've found it very difficult to question the motives of the grief-stricken," Delp pointed out. "Since we do not know where the killers are, it makes it a struggle to predict where he is."

"How far behind the killers was Mr. Harrod?" she asked.

Delp lifted an eyebrow as Arwoods answered, "Three to four minutes."

"That's a long time," she considered. "How would he know where to go?"

"Agent Hubbard," Arwoods responded. "If we knew that answer, we would know where to go."

Delp's phone chirped, and he smiled again. "Excuse me," he said as he stepped away.

Hubbard glanced around the parking lot of the gas station. There were several vehicles, but no other cars. "Chief, how did Detective Delp come upon the scene?"

"He was stopping for gas," he admitted.

Stopping for gas, Hubbard considered. In what?

Delp turned his back away from Hubbard as he spoke into the phone. After a few moments, he hung up and turned back to them.

"Is everything okay, Detective?" she asked.

"Yes, ma'am," he affirmed.

"I'd like to make a quick call, Chief," she addressed Arwoods. "After that, I'd like to get a full debriefing from you."

"Whatever the Miami-Dade Police Department can do to promote national security," he remarked.

Hubbard avoided rolling her eyes. She marched back toward the car, stopping halfway. Hubbard didn't want Vickers any more aware of her thoughts than the local cops. The agent dialed a number.

"It's Hubbard," she said into the phone. "I need background on a Detective Jay Delp with the Palm Beach County Sheriff's Department. Find out what vehicle he drives too. Last, he just received a phone call about two minutes ago. Find out who called him and from where."

She waited a second for the person on the other end to say something.

"I need it now," she confirmed. "Send me the email."

She hung up and turned back toward the two men.

FOURTEEN

T he kid slowly stood up. From the way he held his side, I guessed he had a broken rib. Did Caleb do that? It made little sense. Why would he just beat this kid when he tortured the other one?

Desperation flooded the guy's eyes, and I saw his plan before he made his move. He bolted past me—or rather tried to. My left foot caught him across the shin, and the *Serpiente* face-planted into the gravel. I pivoted on my left foot as soon as it touched the drive, kneeling as I did so, my right knee pressed against the small of his back. The muzzle of the Heckler & Koch pressed against the back of his neck, just above his C7 vertebrae.

"If I pull this trigger, the hollow point round will sever your spine from your head," I pointed out. "There's a good chance you'll live long enough to see everything as your head rolls away from your body. Wouldn't that be cool?"

I didn't believe that was even possible, but it sounded freaky enough to send shivers down my spine. I hoped it conveyed the same feeling to him.

"Sorry," he muttered into the ground. "I won't do anything."

With my left hand, I frisked him, pulling a forty-five out of his waistband. "Were you hiding?" I asked.

His head moved slightly in a nod. I tossed the gun toward the swamp so that it landed in the grass. If it was the weapon this shithead used to murder Caleb's wife, the cops were going to need it.

"I'm going to let you up, but understand me—I'll shoot you in a second. Got it?"

Another quick nod, and I pushed up off his back and rocked into a standing position.

"Let's start with your name?" I demanded.

"Gaspar Castro," he replied, crawling onto his knees.

"Who beat you up?" I asked.

He rose to his feet without answering.

"The same guy who killed your friends?" I questioned.

He didn't answer, but his eyes twitched.

"If you don't want to talk, I got no use for you," I explained.

"No," Castro stated. "It wasn't him."

"He didn't see you out here?"

Castro shook his head, letting it droop forward slightly.

"You got lucky, didn't you?"

He turned his eyes back up to me. I suppose he didn't get the irony.

"You killed the mother, didn't you?" I asked, staring down the barrel of the H&K.

Castro's eyes widened.

"Tell me what happened here?"

"I was back here when it happened. Never heard him pull up, but there was a gunshot. Before I could come to help, Lonzo was screaming in pain. He was crying. I hid behind the barrels."

"Mighty brave of you," I retorted.

"I didn't wanna get killed," he argued.

"I guess that makes sense," I affirmed. "This was an actual threat. Someone who might just as well kill you as look at you."

He nodded.

"Not like an unarmed mother and a kid."

He blinked.

"I don't feel a lot of sympathy for you or your friends," I explained. "If you're lucky, you'll get out of this with a prison sentence."

Castro swallowed.

"I guess if you're unlucky, the dad will get another shot at you."

He shook his head.

"If you think you escaped, I'd think again," I suggested. "How long did it take him to find you? An hour and a half? Hell, it only took me a couple. I'm not nearly as motivated as he is."

"What does he want?" Castro stammered.

"Besides gutting you?" I asked. "Probably his daughter?"

"I don't have her," he admitted.

"But you did," I corrected. "Where is she now?"

"Uh, the father took her," he lied.

"I don't think so," I snapped, stepping toward him with the barrel of the H&K wavering in front of his face. "He wouldn't have bothered torturing your friend if she was here. I don't think he'd want her to see that."

Castro swallowed again. His eyes shifted past me, hoping help would show up.

"Let's try again," I urged.

"Xavier took her," he offered. "He's going to sell her."

"Sell her?" My face contorted. "What do you mean? She's a baby."

His head shook again, back and forth. "He was talking to Lonzo about it."

"Where did he go?" I demanded.

"I don't know," he told me. "Really."

"Let me rephrase that." I pushed the muzzle against his left eye. "Guess."

"He might go to the church," Castro suggested. "I don't think he'd keep the girl there. He'd end up taking her to the boathouse."

"Church?" I questioned. "Boathouse?"

He nodded. "Maybe," he amended.

"Where are they?"

"The church is in Everglades City. It's *Las Serpientes* club. They meet there."

"They?" I asked, grabbing the arm with the coiled viper around it. "You look like a damned snake."

"I mean the board. Xavier, Timon, Carlos, and the others."

"Xavier is the boss?" I asked.

"*El presidente*," he answered.

"Is that an elected position?" I quipped.

Castro stared at me, missing the humor.

"Where's the boathouse?"

Castro shook his head again. "I don't know."

"Why would you say it?" I pressed him. "Why would Xavier take the girl there and not the church?"

"It's in the swamp somewhere," Castro explained. "I've never been there. Some of the other guys talked about it. They bring things in there to avoid the heat."

"Things from overseas?" I asked.

He stared at me.

"Like drugs?"

Castro nodded.

"Women?"

Another nod.

"Who can actually answer my questions?"

"Someone higher than me," Castro admitted.

"Come on," I ordered, pushing him through the door into the garage area.

A different woman sang a sultry song. The slow tempo and smoky voice seemed appropriate for the walk through death we were making. Castro froze when he turned to see the boy hanging from the drill press. Lonzo, I reminded myself.

"Where are you taking me?" he asked.

"Did you see the father leave?" I asked.

He shook his head. "I heard him. He took Xavier's motorcycle."

"Ballsy," I remarked. "What kind of bike does he have?"

Castro shrugged. "A Harley. I don't know what kind."

I sighed. Nothing is ever easy.

On the far side of the garage was a storage locker. I pointed toward it, and Castro obediently shuffled in that direction.

"Get in," I ordered.

He turned to argue, but paused when he found the muzzle staring back at him. He opened the locker, finding it full of car parts stacked on the shelves.

"There's not enough room," he insisted.

"I'll give you fifteen seconds to clean it out," I stated. "After that, I'll shoot you, fold you, and stuff your ass in there."

He scrambled forward, dragging starters, alternators, and an array of gears and belts onto the floor.

"The shelves?" he implored once all the parts were on the floor.

My left foot shot up and kicked the bottom shelf. The metal piece bounced up, dislodging the one above it before falling to the ground. Castro pulled the shelves out.

"Get in," I repeated. This time, he squeezed into the space at the bottom of the locker. It was a tight fit, with his knees pressed against his chest.

Without a word, I slammed the locker shut. This was one of those heavy-duty shipping lockers, and when I slid the bars over to seal it up, there wasn't much chance of him getting out without some help from the outside.

The phone startled me as it rang. I slipped the H&K under my waistband and pulled the phone out of my pocket. A D.C. area code—Shaw.

"General," I answered.

"Lieutenant, you have a knack unlike anyone I've ever known," the general remarked. "You dig up more shit than a damned dung beetle."

"Yes, sir," I replied. "It's a gift."

"Caleb Saunders," she stated, and my brain immediately recognized the last name. "Saunders dropped off the grid. From what I found, the Corps discharged him after basic."

"Discharged?"

"That's what this very thin file tells me."

"Isn't that odd?" I questioned.

"Not that strange. Lots of times there are extenuating circumstances. Although usually there is a mention of those circumstances in the record. Here, there is nothing."

"He was a Marine for a minute then," I commented.

"If you can say that," she added. "There's more though."

I perked up.

"An AFIS search flagged his file. I suppose the local cops ran his prints."

"Probably," I admitted.

"Well, that search also triggered another file. One, I am cleared to see."

"I don't suppose you can tell me about it?" I asked.

"You, Lieutenant, did not have the clearance when you were still on active duty," she remarked. "Suffice it to say, this file is even thinner."

Thin files are often a clear sign that someone has gone to some lengths to omit data. People gather paperwork. For me, there would be my recruiting paperwork, assignments, orders, disciplinary actions, commendations, awards, and discharge papers. That doesn't even touch the physicals. If this file on Caleb was so thin, it's likely because someone didn't want to fill it.

"How deep is this shit pile?" I asked.

"I worry that if you decide to stay in it, Caleb Saunders will be the least of your problems."

As I stared at two of the three bodies Caleb had left here, I wondered what was on the way.

"Thank you, General," I told her.

"Lieutenant, I'm very serious," she warned. "This is some murky water here. Watch your six."

"Yes, sir."

She hung up without another word. I stared at the phone. Her warning still rang in my ears. Shaw wasn't one to shrink from much. I had to wonder what would garner that kind of reaction.

While I had the phone out, I dialed Jay's number.

"Delp," he answered after several rings.

"It's me," I told him. "I found the carjackers."

"Flash, I never doubted you," he replied in a flat tone.

"Don't get too excited," I advised. "Caleb or Harrod—whichever one you're calling him—got to them first."

"Are they down?" he asked.

"One is. Along with what I guess is the guy stripping the cars. I've got the other shooter on ice for now."

"Caleb?"

"In the wind," I reported. "It seems the head of *Las Serpientes* took his daughter from here. The kid's a girl, by the way. From what I got out of the other shooter—his name's Gaspar Castro—they plan to sell the girl."

"Sell her?" Jay asked with the same surprise in his voice that I had. "She's too young."

"I wish that were true," I responded. "We know that's not always the case. I think Caleb is going after Xavier."

"Xavier?" he questioned.

"*El Presidente de Las Serpientes*," I said. "I spoke with Shaw. She filled in very little about him. His last name was Saunders."

"Damn, that's right," he exclaimed.

"Apparently, the Corps discharged him after Parris Island."

"He never finished with us," Jay interjected.

"I know, but the Corps says he did. There's another file that Shaw couldn't share with me. Whatever it was must have given her the willies, 'cause she gave me a stern warning to watch my six."

"Ah," he expressed some realization by dragging the word out a couple of extra syllables. "That might explain the Fed that just showed up looking to talk to the father."

"Fed?"

"An Agent Hubbard with Homeland Security. At least that's what her badge says. She's got a pit bull she left in the car. I don't know his story."

"What do we do, Jay?" I asked. "Caleb is about to take on an entire motorcycle gang."

"Can't really blame him," my friend pointed out.

"He's not really a Marine," I added.

"Flash, that didn't really matter to you."

"Can you find out what the Fed wants with him?" I asked. "Without putting yourself into too much trouble."

"You are going after him?" Jay questioned.

"We need to find his daughter," I answered. "You need to get the cops here."

"Wait," Jay interrupted me. "I can't give them this. They'll know you are off the range with my permission."

"I don't have a range," I quipped.

"You know what I mean."

"Ten-four. I got it covered," I promised him before hanging up.

FIFTEEN

Hubbard's phone rang, interrupting her as she watched the video surveillance behind the counter for the third time. She'd walked the scene just as many times. Arwoods and his deputies had already picked apart the crime scene, but she wasn't ready to let them all go. As long as Arwoods and Delp were hamstringing her, she'd use all of her authority to drag it out for them. Arwoods had grown visibly antsy. He was lighting the sixth Marlboro Light she'd seen since her arrival.

Delp, on the other hand, had an eerily calm demeanor. He hadn't moved from his position, leaning against the column under the fuel island's awning. His arms crossed his chest as he watched her walk around. Arwoods couldn't go anywhere—this was his territory. But Delp just hung around. Why?

"Hubbard," she announced into the phone.

The voice on the other end reported, "I have that information for you."

"Go ahead," Hubbard commanded as she cut her eyes toward the Lincoln, where Vickers waited.

"Jay Delp is the Chief of Detectives for the Palm Beach County Sheriff's Office. It's a position he's only held a couple of months. Prior to that, he'd been with the department for only two years. He transferred from the police department in Panama City, Florida. He was a sniper in Marine Recon before that."

"The Corps?" Hubbard noted.

"Yeah, he's loaded with commendations."

"Were you able to trace the call he got?" Hubbard questioned.

"It was a prepaid number," the woman on the other end explained.

"Could you trace it?"

"Of course," the woman replied snidely.

"If anyone could to it, it was you, Angie," Hubbard praised with a grin.

"It's about forty-five minutes from your location. Looks like a storage place called Complete Storage Needs. It's on Highway 41, just west of you."

"Could you send me the address?" she asked.

"Already did it, Lee," Angie informed her. "Can I do anything else for you?"

"Can you tell me what they talked about?" Hubbard queried.

Angie chuckled, "If only."

"I assumed as much," Hubbard admitted. "But a girl can hope."

"What are you after?" Angie asked.

"Something Carl doesn't want to get out," she admitted. "He tasked me with Vickers."

"Vickers?" the woman on the other end of the phone exclaimed. "He's like a last resort."

"Yeah, Carl's desperate," Hubbard acknowledged.

"Carl's a dumb fuck," Angie said. "He's showing his hand."

"I'll keep my eyes open," Hubbard explained. "If this is as big a fuck-up as I suspect, I can stash it in a back pocket for another day."

"Watch him, Lee," Angie warned. "Carl Winston wouldn't have a problem letting Vickers drop you in the middle of a swamp to fend for yourself."

"If Vickers dropped me, there wouldn't be much I could fend off," she confirmed.

"Be careful, baby," Angie warned.

"I'm always careful," Hubbard told her.

Angie laughed. "Hurry home," she said before disconnecting.

Hubbard slipped the phone in her pocket before walking out to Delp and Arwoods.

"I've got a lead on your guys," she announced.

Arwoods tossed his cigarette toward the street. What kind of idiot smokes around gas pumps? Hubbard watched it land on the asphalt.

"What do you have?" Arwoods asked.

"Why don't we drive out there?" she suggested. "Detective Delp, you could tag along with me if you want."

Delp still hadn't moved from the pole he seemed to support. "Where are we going?"

"Oh, let me make it a surprise," she offered with a wry grin. Her head turned as she made a pretense of surveying the lot. "You don't have a ride anyway, do you?"

"I suppose I can go along for a bit."

"I hope you don't mind the back seat," she added. "It's a little tight."

"No ma'am, I've been in cramped places before."

"No doubt," she acknowledged as she started for the Lincoln. "Just follow us, Chief Arwoods."

Hubbard didn't give Arwoods a chance to respond, and the Chief of Detectives stood dumbfounded for a few seconds before running to his car.

The Black Lincoln pulled out onto the road, heading south. Vickers turned and looked at the newcomer in the back seat.

"Vickers, this is Chief of Detectives Jay Delp."

The man in the front seat locked eyes with Delp silently before turning back to stare out the windshield.

"Why you are a delight," Delp remarked with his folksy tone.

Vickers didn't respond.

"You'll have to forgive Vickers, Detective Delp," Hubbard pointed out. "He isn't as personable as I am."

"Oh, no worries, ma'am," he assured her. "I've handled my fair share of grumpy gators."

Vickers registered nothing.

Hubbard asked, "Was that down here, Detective, or while you were in Panama City?"

"Checking up on me?" he quipped with a wide grin. "You could have just asked. But to your question. A little of both. Even met a few in the Corps."

"You were a Marine?" she asked.

"Well, if you checked on me, you already know that," he stated. He leaned forward, so he was almost over Vickers's shoulder. "Recon."

Vickers turned his head slowly until he was just inches from Delp's. Neither man said anything for several seconds before Delp leaned back in the seat.

"Why don't you tell me about you, Agent Hubbard?" he asked.

"Nothing to tell," she explained. "Certainly nothing that would pertain to this case."

"Hmm," Delp mused.

"Why do I feel you are keeping something from me, Detective Delp?"

"Agent Hubbard, I don't know what you mean," he oozed. "But I'll tell you the truth. I've been married a few times, but that doesn't mean I'm not open to doing it again."

The woman made a curt nod.

"Why don't you tell me where we are going?" Delp asked.

"It's a solid lead," she admitted. "We traced something to a storage unit not too far away. Might be a good place to hide a stolen car."

"A storage unit?" Delp commented. "Makes sense. How did you trace it so quickly? Does the CIA have some tracking device embedded in our vehicles now?"

"No," she chuckled. "Besides, I told you I'm with Homeland Security. The CIA doesn't work domestically."

"Right," he mocked. "And strippers really want to get to know me."

Her eyes cut to the rearview mirror connecting with his. They were deep blue, and she had to admit they were nice. Compared to the black eyes of Vickers or Winston's shit-brown eyes, Delp's offered a trusted assurance. Of course, he was lying to her. But somehow he was aware she knew he was lying. What did that make it? Angie would call it diplomacy, but she understood the level of bullshit filling all levels of bureaucracy.

Not that Hubbard didn't comprehend it. In fact, she navigated the steaming piles like she was sailing through an archipelago. No, this was different. Delp was involved. Hubbard leaned toward the Marine angle. She wanted to delve a little deeper into the detective. Take a hard look at his military record. See if Corsair had crossed paths with Delp at some point. She'd text Angie and get a complete copy of his OFMP.

"Have y'all been down to this part of Florida before?" Delp questioned from the back.

"I've been to Miami," Hubbard responded. "Down to Key West too."

Vickers didn't respond. At some point, Hubbard considered, Delp was going to question her partner's demeanor.

"This ain't quite like Miami," Delp explained. "Once you get in the Glades, it's an unusual mix. Plenty of tourists. They never stray far from the paths. Then, you get your locals. Most have businesses down here. Charters, restaurants, that sort of thing. Finally, you get the outcasts. Some of these wander into the swamp to vanish forever. I'd guess there are more bodies dumped in the Glades than any other body of water—not counting the ocean."

"Trying to intimidate me, Detective Delp?" Hubbard questioned.

"Not at all," he promised. "Just conversating."

"Do you know Thomas Harrod?" Hubbard asked him.

Delp's head made a slow arc back and forth as he replied, "No, ma'am. I can't say that I do."

"What about Caleb Saunders?"

"Who is that?" Delp asked in response.

Her eyes locked with his again. "I figure we'll find out pretty soon," she remarked.

He shrugged nonchalantly. Nothing seemed to bother him. Vickers was the same, but at least Delp wrapped his demeanor in congeniality and that Southern twang.

"Where are you from, Detective?" she asked.

"Originally, I grew up in Ocean Springs, Mississippi."

"Where is that?"

"Just across the bay from Biloxi. They got casinos and beaches with the brownest water you've ever seen on any coast."

"Brown?"

He shrugged again. "It's still a beach."

"Why is it brown?"

"I suspect it's a fine mixture of the muddy bottom in the Mississippi Sound and the billions of gallons of dirty Delta water the Mississippi River dumps into the Gulf only fifty miles west."

"Sounds lovely," she said with a curled lip.

"What about you, Agent Hubbard? Where are you from?"

"D.C."

"I didn't think anyone was from D.C.," he commented.

"Some of us are."

"And Agent Vickers?"

Vickers turned his head and stared at Delp.

"You are a hell of a conversationalist, Vickers," Delp quipped.

Hubbard touched the brakes as the address Angie gave her was coming up. A sign reading, "Complete Storage Needs" loomed ahead. The black Lincoln pulled through the open gate. Hubbard did a double-take as they drove through the opening, which was shaking back and forth as if the automatic opener was stuck in a cycle. Arwoods followed behind her in his unmarked cruiser.

"This is Collier County," Arwoods announced as he got out of his cruiser. "Just barely, but not in my jurisdiction."

"Don't worry, Chief," Hubbard assured him. "I don't think Detective Delp has been in his jurisdiction all day."

Hubbard marched toward the office, which obviously once was an old gas station. The air conditioning blasted her as she pushed through the door. Arwoods and Delp stepped in behind her.

"Oh!" Arwoods exclaimed when he saw the body slumped over the desk. The Chief of Detectives whipped out his Glock 22.

Hubbard pulled her Kel Tec PF-9 from her holster. She spun around on her heel and glared at Delp. "Chief Arwoods, you might want to call this in," she remarked. "Delp, why don't you and I check out the rest of the property?"

When they were back outside, she looked at the detective. "You want to tell me what's going on?"

"I expect you know more than I do at this point," Delp answered.

Hubbard stared at him pointedly. "Why don't you tell me who called you earlier?" she questioned.

He lifted an eyebrow. "I suspect you pulled some Patriot Act shit with me already," he said. "Why don't you tell me who you think called me?"

"I can't figure it out yet," she answered, leading him between the buildings. Somewhere faint music echoed between the metal buildings. "I'm thinking you know Thomas Harrod. If you're just looking the other way, I can't blame you. Those shitheads deserve whatever comes to them."

"I don't know Thomas Harrod," Delp stated.

"Caleb Saunders?" she asked.

"You still haven't told me who that is," he told her.

"I don't have to, though. Do I?" she asked. "Is that who called you? Did Saunders kill that guy back there? Even if I think he's justified, it doesn't make it legal. He'll do time for this. You don't want to let him take you down, too."

"As I understand it," Delp commented, "you think Thomas Harrod is this Caleb Saunders. What's your interest in either of them?"

"National Security," she stated flatly as she followed the sound of the music.

"Could you be a little more generic?" he quipped.

"Have better clearance," she advised, stepping around the corner. Her Kel Tec raised up when she was facing the open units. Spanish music filtered out.

"That looks like the Mercedes you're looking for," she pointed out. "Guess Saunders already found them."

Hubbard pointed to the body on the floor.

"Did you hear that?" Delp asked, pausing in the middle of the makeshift garage.

"What?"

"Sounded like a thud," he remarked.

She heard it again, coming from a shipping locker against the wall. Around the door, auto parts lay scattered haphazardly on the ground, as if someone tossed them out hastily. Her gun came up, and Delp raised his hand, signaling her to let him open the locker. He grabbed the lever which operated the door assembly. The two metal doors creaked as they swung open, and a Latino man tumbled out onto the floor.

SIXTEEN

On the corner of Collier Avenue and Datura Street, an old white church sat. Its short steeple still towered higher than most of the town. Originally, the Everglades City Missionary Baptist Church constructed the old building in 1946. They worshiped there until 1960, when most of the congregation migrated elsewhere following the flooding and destruction left by Hurricane Donna. As if ordained by God, the structure survived the storm as it ravaged across Collier County, but the damage left it abandoned for the next twenty years. In the mid-eighties, the original congregation resurged. They renovated the building and occupied the church until Hurricane Andrew sent the remaining congregants scattering. Again, the structure remained despite water and wind damage. In 1999, a shell company named SCH Inc purchased the building and the lot it was on. After renovations, SCH Inc. leased the building to Daniel Estrada for one hundred years. At the time, Estrada was the president of *Las Serpientes*. In 2008, Xavier Jimenez assumed both leadership of the motorcycle club along with the lease for the building.

Since Las Serpientes began their occupation of the church, they removed the pews and converted the baptistry into a hot tub. At the center of the room, a bar filled in the area around the pulpit. The crucifix that once adorned the front of the podium had long vanished, to be replaced with an intricately carved relief of Quetzalcoatl, a Mayan god depicted as a feathered serpent. An identical image of Quetzalcoatl hung from the ceiling on a banner. *Las Serpientes* converted the inside from a house of worship into something more resembling a roadhouse bar. One side of the former church had individual rooms built to operate as classrooms. Now, the rooms once used to teach preschool kids the names of the twelve apostles were bedrooms for several of the club members. The office at the front of the church now held the "temple," where Xavier and the top members of the club managed the affairs of *Las Serpientes*.

In the corner of the open bar area, Amanda Harrod sat at a table alone. She had a half-eaten Hot Pocket in front of her and a glass bottle of Coca-Cola. Her fingers poked at the cheese and pepperoni sticking out of the microwaved meal. Her eyes stayed down as the man who brought her here talked at another table.

Xavier Jimenez leaned back in the chair. The two men across from him leaned over the table with stern faces. Both wore denim jackets with the sleeves cut off. The frayed ends of cotton around the hole were brown with age. A small patch with the same feathered serpent deity was sewn over the left breast pocket on each jacket. The thicker man on the right sported a thick mustache under a crooked nose that someone broke more than once. The other was slender and tall with a beard, braided and bound, that hung down to his chest.

"What the hell were they thinking?" Silva, the mustached one, snapped.

"They fucked up," Xavier acknowledged. "What do we do with her?"

Silva shook his head. "I don't like the idea of killing a kid."

Xavier nodded. "Agreed."

The other man commented, "We can't keep her around here."

"I know, Tomas," Xavier replied.

Tomas continued, "If the cops find anything to tie those two to the murders, it will be a matter of time before the Feds come sniffing around."

"I'm going to take her to the boathouse," Xavier explained. "But she can't stay there forever."

Silva lifted his head. "What about Khaled?"

"The Libyan?" Tomas questioned.

"He has connections outside of America," Silva suggested with a shrug. "If we get her out of the country, the Feds will have a hard time tracking her."

Xavier folded his arms across his chest. His brown eyes drifted off for a second. Finally, he told Silva, "Call him. I want her out of the country."

Tomas shook his head solemnly. "That Arab bastard might keep her. He'd like a little white girl."

"I don't care," Xavier stated. "We need her gone yesterday."

"Got it," Silva told him.

Xavier stood up. "All right, brothers, I'll be off-grid until I get her dropped. Angel and Camilla can handle her until Khaled comes to get her."

"You want him to go to the boathouse?" Silva asked.

"No, he can get her out at the drop point. I'll have Angel take her out there."

Silva nodded.

Xavier walked to the girl. "Come with me," he insisted.

"Where's my mama?" she asked.

"I'm going to take you to her," he told her.

The girl stared up at him with distrustful eyes.

"I promise," he assured her.

"Where?"

"She and your daddy went out on a boat," he lied. "Do you like boats?"

Her chin wagged slowly. "Jackson, too?"

"Yes, Jackson is there too."

"He wanted to see the algaters."

Xavier smiled. "Exactly. They took him to see the alligators. You weren't big enough to go yet, so I'm going to take you now."

Her face still questioned the man, but she didn't know what else to do. "'Kay," she agreed.

The club president took Amanda by the hand and led her to the door. "We have to go to the boat," he explained.

Half a block west from the church was a wooded lot on the banks of Lake Placid. Xavier bought the land a few years ago under his own name. It flooded too often to build anything on it, but it was perfect for a small dock. Several of the club members had boats on the dock.

Xavier escorted Amanda by the hand as they walked along the narrow dirt path toward the water. The girl didn't speak as they stepped onto the pier.

At the end of the pier was Xavier's 2012 Hartline Airboat.

"Have you ever seen a boat like this?" he asked the girl.

She shook her head, staring at the giant fan mounted on the stern of the vessel.

"The water down here can get too shallow for a motor, so this propeller works just like a fan in your house. It pushes the air behind the boat and that pushes the boat forward. I can drive through extremely shallow water with this."

She nodded, but whether she understood what he was trying to explain, he couldn't tell. As long as she was calm, it would make things easier.

"Well, it makes a lot of noise," he explained, preparing her for the roar the engine made. "Are you ready for that?"

Another nod.

Xavier climbed down the ladder hanging off the pier and stepped into the boat. He reached up and lifted Amanda Harrod off the dock, setting her in the boat.

"Put this on," he ordered, handing her an orange over-the-head life vest. The girl complied, and Xavier snapped the jacket. If they spotted a ranger out here, there was less of the chance of being stopped if the kid was wearing a life jacket.

"Sit there," he told her, pointing to the chair in the front. "It has a seat belt."

The engine blared as Xavier turned the key. He pulled the looped dock lines off the pier and pushed away from the wooden pylons. He pushed the throttle down slowly as he adjusted the rudders on the fan, turning the bow of the boat away from the shoreline. Slowly, he increased speed as he took a heading across the lake.

He always found the idea of calling this a lake somewhat ludicrous. Now, while it was in the wet season, the water was deeper, but it still wasn't over six feet anywhere. As he pushed toward the mangroves, he followed the narrowing channel through the trees. While Everglades City wasn't much of an urban area, it took less than five minutes to vanish from civilization. It could have been the Amazon rainforest for all anyone would know. A green canopy of leaves blocked the sun, cooling the area. But the downside to the shade anywhere in Florida but especially in the Glades was the bugs. Mosquitoes swarmed the cooler areas, and they seemed to love the shade. Unfortunately, the trees also blocked the breeze which only seemed to give the blood-suckers an advantage.

He kept the throttle about halfway down. The channel made sharp turns and cuts as it meandered through the swamp. The airboat didn't have brakes, and if he drove too fast, he risked losing control in a turn or hitting a submerged log only to ricochet out of control. Better to keep it slow and avoid crashing into the trees. In a few minutes, he'd be outside of the range of any cell tower. His VHF radio would be his only communication if he got into trouble. That had its shortcomings—the signal would only be received by someone within range. Even then, the person on the other end might be fifty miles away, unable to reach him.

He didn't really mind that, though. The Everglades offered the ultimate in self-reliance. It tested him every time he ventured into it.

He glanced down at the girl. She stared ahead blankly. Xavier guessed she was three. Old enough to communicate. He remembered his kids at that age. He didn't live with Lucia, but he was still involved. Not that he was ever the guy to coach the kid's football team.

Xavier spotted an alligator gliding along the surface. If they aren't moving, it is far more difficult to spot them. He'd seen enough of them while out here to know what to look for, but most of the other guys didn't realize how close they were. It was often part of the hazing for new patches—get a newbie close to one and scare the piss out of him.

The rudders on the rear swiveled, shifting the direction of the bow starboard so the Hartline could hug the tree line as it curved around. The ride out to the boathouse usually took about ninety minutes. He'd made the trip hundreds of times now. While some of the other members used their chart plotters to wind through the maze of mangroves and creeks, he knew the way in the dark. Even after the annual flooding washed out half the markers he once used to judge his turns, he knew the path.

It was literally a path. Once the channel he was going down narrowed, he slipped into Halfway Creek, which might have a foot of water in the dry season. Now it would be three or four feet deep and easy to navigate. If the winter was too dry, he might have to come around the coast to Turner River and find his way through. It added two hours to the trip, so he was always grateful to the high waters.

The boathouse was little more than an old fishing cabin on stilts. It was one of hundreds out in the middle of the Glades. Some were long abandoned. Others had occupants who wanted to hide from the world out here. Xavier heard about the boathouse from his predecessor. At that time, it was nothing more than a fishing shack. Xavier carried several members out with lumber and tools. When they finished, the cabin was more than livable, but comfortable. A 3500-watt generator coupled with a

2000-watt battery bank offered plenty of power.

Over the last eight years, the mangroves around the house were carefully trimmed to hide the building. This was a section of the Glades so far off the beaten path that even the locals didn't come out here. Only once did they have a visitor. A kayaker who wandered too far east and thought the stilted building would make a good campsite. Unfortunately, three Guatemalan women that *Las Serpientes* smuggled into Florida occupied the house. Angel, who spent most of his time out here, had to drag the kayak and the body back toward one of the campgrounds so there wouldn't be a search near the boathouse.

The girl began fidgeting around. It had surprised him she lasted this long. Her head turned back toward him a couple of times. Xavier thought she might have said something, but her tiny voice couldn't overcome the decibels created by the airboat's motor. If he ignored her for a bit, she might be okay. They were getting closer to their destination. Ten minutes by Xavier's guess.

The final cut was barely visible as Xavier slowed the motor. There had once been an old milk jug attached to a tree to mark the entrance, but one day it was gone. Xavier didn't replace it. By now, the few who traveled out here knew the location. If not, they had the route saved on their individual GPS.

The bow of the boat pushed the mangrove branches aside as it pressed through the growth. Xavier watched the girl as she shrank back from the sinewy green arms stretching across the boat. He touched the machete strapped to the seat. It didn't happen often, but there had been a time or two that the boat's passage dislodged a snake sleeping in the branches. Most of the time, the reptile slithered over the side, trying to escape, but once the damned thing panicked, coiling up and prepared to strike. A swift strike with the machete ended the threat.

Luckily, they passed through without incident. Trees opened up to a small clearing. Yellowish algae covered the surface. On the opposite side of the clearing, Xavier saw the boathouse. Mangroves and vines covered the outside, obscuring it, however, the round shape stood out clearly to him.

He eased the Hartline between the stilts until the hull nudged up against the wooden platform. As he dropped off the raised seat, he scooped up the dock line and wound it around the aluminum cleat. After moving forward, he attached the bow line to the dock.

The girl stared at him.

"How did you like the ride?" he asked.

She shrugged. "Where's Mama?" she questioned.

"She'll be here later," he lied. "Let's go up and you can meet my friends."

Amanda Harrod shimmied her butt until she slid off the seat. Xavier lifted her onto the wooden dock before climbing out.

A wooden staircase spiraled up to a deck. A heavy rope stretched along the stairwell, acting as a makeshift handrail. Xavier took Amanda's hand in his right hand and led her up the stairs.

The upper deck had a wooden railing with dark netting surrounding it to keep the mosquitoes and other flying insects away from the occupants. Xavier pushed through the overlapping net to step into the protected area.

A brute stepped through the door. Long black hair curled up on his shoulders. A thick black beard grew wild about his face. The dark Guatemalan skin underneath the facial hair leathered from days in the sun.

"X, what's up?" he greeted Xavier by slinging his open hand out and grabbing Xavier's. The two came together for an embrace before stepping back.

"Angel, how are things out here?" Xavier asked.

"Quiet," he replied.

"Is that Xavier?" a husky feminine voice called from inside the shack.

"Yeah, *mi amor*," Angel shouted back.

A twenty-something woman stepped through the door. A thin cotton dress hung off her shoulders, barely stretching to her thighs. Her brown skin appeared smooth and soft. A wide grin flashed across her face.

"Hey baby," Xavier greeted her before pulling her close to kiss her lips. "How is this asshole treating you?"

"Like a goddess," she assured him. Her eyes turned down to see Amanda standing shyly behind Xavier. "Who is this?" she asked, kneeling down to stare into the girl's white face. "What's your name?"

"'Manda," the girl responded.

"Amanda?"

The girl nodded.

"I'm Camilla," the woman told her. "Do you want a cookie?"

Another nod, and Camilla took the girl by the hand, leading her into the cabin.

"Who is she, X?" Angel asked.

"Gaspar jacked her family's car. The asshole didn't know the girl was in the car seat."

"Dumbass," Angel commented.

"Silva's going to put a call into Khaled over in Miami. We need to move her. There's probably an alert out already."

"No one will find her here," Angel assured him. "When does he want her?"

"No idea," Xavier explained. "I'll let you know. You can meet him out at the regular rendezvous."

Angel nodded.

"Do you guys need anything?" the president asked.

"Camilla's got a list," he told him. "Some soap, milk, some other things."

"If we can move the girl soon, I'll get it out in the next couple of days."

"You gonna stay long?" Angel asked.

"No, I think if I slip off, it might be easier with the girl. She has asked about her mother a lot, but I've put her off."

Angel nodded. "We can manage it," he promised.

"I figure you mean Camilla can manage it," Xavier quipped.

Angel smiled.

SEVENTEEN

From under the brush, Caleb Saunders stared across the way to the white church building. The exterior paint was recent, probably within the last six months. They'd simply painted over the flaking remnants, leaving bulging globs on the siding. Sand, broken coral, and empty Pacifico cans littered the bare ground around the building. A carved snake sculpture stood about four feet tall as he arrived. The safest approach had been on foot through the surrounding yards. It was nearing dusk, and the shadows from the trees grew long across the grass.

Something moved past his foot. A frog, he thought without moving.

If they had Amanda inside the church, charging in with his gun out wouldn't be prudent. When the sun set, he planned to reconnoiter the church. By now, word of what happened at the garage might have gotten to the members of *Las Serpientes*. He didn't think so. From what the kid told him, the boss left with Amanda. There would be no reason for him to contact the chop shop. No way to know. His best option was to prepare for it. He'd seen jobs go sideways for crazier things. It only takes one person to show up and gum up the works.

Certainly, that shithead didn't call in, he mused with some satisfaction. People like *Las Serpientes* considered themselves invulnerable. Mostly that was true. Caleb assumed the club held local law enforcement at bay, probably with payoffs and threats. It seemed they spread their illegalities around. Sure, cops might bust the chop shop, but he saw nothing tying it to this building. In fact, it took an extreme amount of pressure to encourage that kid to talk. Unfortunately for him, Caleb mastered applying that kind of pressure. Most people didn't have the stomach for an interrogation like that. Law enforcement certainly didn't operate that way.

Las Serpiente may remain mostly insulated from law enforcement. However, even rats penetrated the most well-built houses out all the time. And Caleb Saunders was the biggest rodent problem the motorcycle club would ever see.

Corsair had nothing. These snakes took his wife and children.

Over the past ten years, a consistent thought occurred to him. He'd heard other dads moan about the loss of freedom. The wife and kids tied them down. He never felt that way. To say his family tied him down might be accurate. Audrey leashed him. Jackson and Amanda restrained him. They kept him grounded. Comfortable. Domesticated.

Those two thugs cut the only chain keeping
Caleb Saunders in check. They killed Thomas
Harrod and resurrected Caleb Saunders.

Now, they found themselves forced to face
Corsair.

His attention drew to a man with a Saddam
Hussein-style mustache exiting the church.
The Latino man climbed onto a gold Harley
Davidson Low Rider. The V-twin engines
roared, echoing down the street. Caleb considered grabbing Hussein for a little conversation,
but the evening was still too bright. If he gave
away his position too soon, he might endanger
Amanda. Hussein rumbled past with no idea
he'd escaped anything.

Caleb listened as the timbre of the bike lingered in the air until Hussein got far enough
away. After the sound faded, the neighborhood
quieted again.

He sensed the frog hop off his foot, but Caleb
didn't flinch. He waited. Twenty minutes from
now, the remaining bits of daylight will wane.
He'd wait until night came. A new moon arrived tonight, and absent some street and porch
lights, he'd have complete darkness to move
around.

If he found Amanda inside the church, he
planned to slip inside and get her out. Any
Serpiente that got in his way wouldn't survive,
but her safety took precedence over revenge.
However, after he took Amanda to safety, he'd
come back. *Las Serpientes* might have forgotten
about him by then, but he'd remind them as he
exterminated every member of the club.

If they'd taken Amanda somewhere else, though, he'd find one and make them talk. He didn't know how many members the club had, but if he worked his way through all of them, he'd find his daughter.

As he lay in two feet of grass and brush, a tiny part of him nagged at the rest of him. It didn't seem fair, but he recognized clearly what appeared to be karma. Corsair killed many people during his time with the Office of Compliance. At first, he let his superiors convince him that the targets posed a threat. They had goals or intentions that might not line up with his own country. At some point, Corsair realized there existed a difference between his country and his government. When the distinction grew so great, he walked away. Not before he'd realized how far his actions had gone. Caleb knew the lines he crossed. He vowed he wouldn't cross them again.

Unfortunately for *Las Serpientes*, this didn't constitute a line he vowed not to cross.

A Jeep hauling a center console fishing boat drove past the church. He watched the vehicle as it crept down the street. It seemed too slow. But the streets grew darker. If the driver looked for an address, it might be difficult to make out. Probably a local coming back from his day on the water, Caleb decided.

When the Jeep's taillights vanished, Caleb counted off five minutes in his head. The streets remained empty during that time. He pushed up slowly, certain no eyes were on him, cut cautiously nonetheless. His fingers dug into the ground under him, scooping up a clump of wet earth. Two fingers smeared across his hand before applying the mud to his face.

Caleb still wore the blue golf shirt he'd put on this morning. This morning—when his biggest plan was to make sure Jackson saw an alligator. Had it only been ten hours ago? Ten hours. A lifetime. There was no time to grieve now. Not while he was on a mission.

He crossed the streets. An onlooker might think he'd dressed up for Halloween. The zombie golfer. His bare skin covered in mud. Brown stains covered his pale blue shirt. Some left from the mud, others were the dried blood of the Lonzo kid. Even his hair streaked back with dried dirt and leaves embedded in the strands.

Once he'd crossed the street, the shadows masked him, with the longest run between cover being only fifty feet. Caleb didn't run, though. He moved slowly, without crouching or skulking.

When on mission, the object is stealth. It isn't somewhat different when it's one man versus a squad. A group of soldiers moves quickly and quietly to stay out of sight. A single man can move slower. More deliberate. That technique puts the man closer to his target before he reveals himself. If he even does that. Many men have died without knowing their assassin was next to them.

As Corsair skulked along the side of the church, he kept his back to the wall. In the dark, the man was invisible.

On the back of the church, he found a deck—an addition made by *Las Serpientes*. A small flight of four steps led from the ground to the deck. A single spotlight illuminated the wooden platform where Caleb saw several ashtrays and a plastic garbage can overflowing with beer cans and bottles. Swiftly, Caleb climbed the stairs and walked through the light.

No one noticed.

The door was locked, but Caleb dropped to his knees. The one thing he picked up in the chop shop was a small lock pick set. When he saw it on the table next to the sockets, he pocketed them. He suspected there'd be a need for them at some point.

Lock picks weren't something Tom Harrod would have worried about. He didn't need to get in and out of places without drawing attention. He'd thrived as a contractor, barely using even the tools needed for building the structures he oversaw. It was mostly reading blueprints and scheduling others. In retrospect, it wasn't much different from what his handlers did in the Office of Compliance.

Caleb hadn't considered his handlers in years, but today he wondered how fast word of his reemergence reached them. It was inevitable, but if he could get to Amanda, there was still time to disappear again.

The worry that one day he'd need to vanish lingered for four or five years. But no one ever came. For the first six months, Caleb expected to see Carl Winston at every corner. Winston wasn't the immediate threat, but once the fact Corsair was alive got out, he expected a Kill-On-Sight order to be issued. That person would not be a familiar face. It would be whatever replacement the OOC found for Corsair. Younger. Stronger, even.

He'd prepped for the day he needed to run. A lock box at a storage place in Atlanta held a go bag with $50,000. There were passports for him, Audrey, and the kids.

Unfortunately, he didn't plan to be seven hundred miles away when the time came. Best laid plans and all.

The lock clicked, and he extracted the pick. Without making a sound, he twisted the knob and pulled the door open a crack. Light spilled through the crack, and he peered inside.

On the other side of the door, Caleb found a kitchen. Empty. He stepped inside, pulling the chrome forty-five he'd taken off the *Caballero*. Men spoke in Spanish somewhere toward the front. A pot of something simmered on the stove. It smelled like fish and hot peppers. He glanced at the soup. Chunks of onions and garlic cloves floated on the surface with some leafy herbs and white meat.

Caleb hadn't eaten since the complimentary continental breakfast this morning. He'd shared a fresh waffle with Jackson and ate a banana. The realization didn't stir any hunger pangs. In fact, the idea of food gnarled his gut, pushing bile up his throat.

Footsteps approached the swinging kitchen door, and Caleb raised the forty-five as a tall Latino man stepped through the door. A long beard covered the man's face, and he'd braided it like a pony tail. Brown eyes widened as he registered the muzzle of the forty-five staring at him. Caleb raised his left finger to his lips, advising the *Serpiente* to remain silent.

"¡Ayuda! Tenemos un..." the man shouted, lunging forward to grab the gun.

Caleb squeezed the trigger, and the explosion from the muzzle obliterated the *Serpiente's* face, sending him falling back as two men raced through the doors.

"Damn it," Caleb cursed, shooting the figure on the right as the other piled into the kitchen.

The third man collided with Caleb, slamming them into the stove. Boiling soup sloshed out, burning both men. Corsair shoved off the stove, throwing the other man back a few inches, enough for the man to pop a front kick up and knocking the chrome pistol from Caleb's hand. The club member balled a fist and swung it toward Caleb. His torso twisted away from the punch, and Caleb drove his fist into the man's ribs. The other man coughed as the blow struck his chest.

Caleb shoved him back, and the man pulled a four-inch hunting knife of a scabbard on his belt. Corsair grabbed the handle of the soup pot and swung the liquid onto the man.

"Ahhh!" he screamed just before the bottom of the hot pot pummeled his head.

Caleb hit him over and over until the man crumpled to the floor. The side of his temple appeared misshapen and flat as the man's eyes glassed over.

He heard the door behind him creak, and Corsair dropped the pot and swept the chrome forty-five up in his hand as the back door swung open. A tall blond man stepped through the door. Caleb raised the barrel of his gun up as the other man leveled a M45 at him.

The new guy didn't fit the bill for a member of a motorcycle club. He was wearing a tank top, shorts, and leather sandals. The blue eyes and blond hair didn't fit the Latino membership, either.

"Who the hell are you?" Caleb demanded.

"Caleb Saunders?" the man questioned.

His face triggered something in Caleb's eidetic memory. His eyes shifted to the man's right shoulder, where a tattoo of a skull with a single boat paddle behind it was inked into his skin.

"Parris Island?" Caleb asked.

"Yeah," the man stated. "You remember me?"

Caleb cocked his head. Had they found him already? That was fast, even for the OOC.

"Wait, Caleb," he pleaded, dropping the barrel of the M45. "I'm not here to hurt you."

"Who are you then?"

"Name's Chase Gordon," he told him. "We were at Parris together."

"Gordon," Caleb commented. The name came back to him. "Call name was Flash?"

"Yeah," Gordon answered. "I'm trying to help you."

A rumble shook the building as if a plane just buzzed the steeple. It took a second for the noise to register. Motorcycles. A lot of them.

"Shit," Gordon muttered.

"Who the hell are you two?" a voice shouted behind Gordon.

Caleb watched as Gordon turned to see two Latino men wearing denim jackets. One held a Mossberg twelve-gauge leveled at the middle of Gordon. The other stared down a .357 Magnum pointed directly at Caleb. At that distance, the Mossberg would probably kill both of them. Even if it didn't, the Magnum would be sure to finish Caleb before he could turn it on either newcomer.

EIGHTEEN

T he man wasn't talking. It was some mis-
guided loyalty to his gang.

She's pulled his sheet. Gaspar Castro. Age
twenty-two. He'd been in trouble with the
law since he was fourteen. Lots of possession
charges—seemed like mostly weed. The local
cops did little for that. The grand theft charge
when he was nineteen put him behind bars
for twelve months. After that, he'd been off the
radar. More likely, he'd gotten better at not getting caught.

Now he was facing a murder charge, and that
might scare him into talking. For now, the kid
was a defense attorney's dream. He refused to
talk to anyone without a lawyer. Only Hubbard didn't want to let him have one yet. She
needed information that even Arwoods and
Delp couldn't be privy to. Now, she had to deal
with another cop, Detective Cheney, with Collier County. Arwoods insisted on playing it by
the book. While the initial murder was in his
county, he wanted to loop in the Collier County
Sheriff's Department to legitimize everything.

And it was a nightmare. Hubbard had seen nothing quite like it. One victim barely reacted before Corsair shot him down. Unfortunately for the other one, he tortured him until he gave him the information he wanted. Once he had that, he pressed the drill bit through the gang member's skull. It was grotesque enough to draw Vickers out of the car. The man studied the scene the way an art student might examine a Van Gogh. She even saw a hint of admiration in his eyes.

Delp stood back out of the way. He wasn't squeamish like Arwoods seemed to be, but he wasn't impressed the way Vickers was. If anything, she might classify it as concerned.

There was one question she had right now. Who locked Gaspar Castro in the locker? If all of their conclusions were correct, Castro was the other shooter. He matched the description of the video. Why would Corsair only beat him to a pulp when he tortured and murdered the other one?

Hubbard walked up to the cruiser where Arwoods had placed Castro after the EMT checked him over.

"I need to talk to him," she stated.

"He's demanding a lawyer still," the Chief of Detectives told her.

"He's not getting one anytime soon," she informed him.

"Cheney's going to want to take him in," Arwoods explained.

"If I have to ship that little bastard to Guantanamo, I will," Hubbard threatened. She wondered if she could justify that, but it sounded threatening. Arwoods didn't strike her as smart enough to call her bluff. Cheney didn't impress her either. He was dumber than Arwoods, and it was obvious that the man was gearing up to run for office someday. He only cared about how it would look.

Vickers now leaned against the black Lincoln and watched them. Hubbard wondered when she was going to put that asshole to any use.

She climbed in the front seat and turned to face Castro. "Gaspar, right?" she asked.

"I ain't saying shit without an attorney," the man stated bluntly.

"You can't have an attorney until we take you in for questioning," she told him. "Let me introduce myself. My name is Lee Hubbard. I'm an agent with Homeland Security. Right now, I'm the best friend you could have."

"Why's that?" he questioned.

"Because I don't give two shits about you or who you killed."

His eyebrows furrowed.

"That's right. You are a teeny tiny fish. I want the whale."

"I ain't talking," he repeated.

"Shut up," she scolded. "I'm not through explaining the situation to you."

"I want the whale, and I don't care what I have to do to get him. Those cops outside—they want to bust you for killing that mother. Can't blame them. You are a worthless piece of shit. At least, mostly worthless."

He shook his head, holding his tongue for the moment.

"I'm sure you didn't do very well in school. Your kind doesn't usually."

"My kind what?" he shouted.

Hubbard reached across the seat to grab a Taser strapped to the dash. Twisting back around, she aimed it through the bars and pushed the button. The leads shot out and attached to Castro, who convulsed violently.

She released the trigger, and Castro's body slumped over in the seat. The dribble of urine running down his leg onto the vinyl floor curled her lip. A second later, the aroma hit her nose. While she waited, she returned the Taser to the clip she'd retrieved it from. Arwoods wouldn't be happy about the condition of his cruiser.

Hubbard didn't care. Castro stirred as he came around.

"Wadufuq!" he mumbled, as if his tongue wasn't functioning properly.

"See, this is how we treat terrorists," she offered with a sly grin.

"Imnouhterrist!"

"The fun thing about my job is that I get to decide if you are a terrorist or not," Hubbard commented. "Are you a legal citizen of the United States of America?"

"Uh," he stammered.

"No, you aren't," she advised. "I can easily revoke your status. It takes one phone call from me. After that, I will have you deported from this country."

He stared at her.

"I know what you're considering now," she suggested. "Is it better to keep your mouth shut and go back to Guatemala, or start talking and paint a target on your back?"

Castro didn't speak.

Hubbard continued, "There is a third option too. I can ship you to Guantanamo for interrogation. You think a little jolt from me is bad. You haven't seen what those guys do down there."

He shook his head. "I'm not a terrorist," he repeated, now that his tongue began to work properly.

"I think Audrey and Jackson Harrod would disagree," she pointed out.

His head continued wagging back and forth, but he couldn't find the right words to defend himself. How did this day get so fucked? It was a simple jacking. This wasn't his first one, and by now he should have a pocket full of cash and be heading to a club with a couple of girls. Now he was wondering how he could get out of this. After the whipping Xavier gave him, he didn't want to rat on him. But this woman wasn't playing. Deportation was bad, but she was threatening to make him vanish altogether. Was she bluffing? He didn't think so. Cops can't just taser a prisoner while they're under arrest.

Maybe he could see what she wants him to say, he considered.

Hubbard watched the man's eyes as these thoughts worked their way around his head. Gaspar Castro weighed his options and didn't like what he was coming up with.

"How about tell me who killed your friends?" she asked, offering an olive branch. "You have to want whoever did that caught before they come back to finish you, right?"

He seemed to think about it before his head barely shifted in a nod.

"Who was it?" she asked again.

"Hell if I know. Some dude. He asked where the girl was."

"The girl?" she questioned. "From the carjacking?"

Gaspar looked at her, realizing he'd talked too much, but feeling like he might as well continue telling Hubbard everything.

"Yeah, we didn't realize she was in the car," he admitted.

Lee Hubbard wanted to smile with satisfaction now that Castro talked. It was just a matter of opening the valve a little. Once a suspect thinks he can give a little, it's too easy for more to spill out.

"You didn't mean to kidnap her, then?" she asked, leading him along.

"No," he confessed. "Lonzo freaked out. Wanted to kill her and dump her in the swamp."

Gaspar Castro dropped his head and shook it slowly. "I couldn't do that. It reminded me of my little sister."

Hubbard listened skeptically as Castro announced his gallant efforts to save this girl only minutes after killing her family. But she let him continue.

"Was it the father than put you in the locker?" she clarified.

"No, I don't know who it was," he explained. "He asked a bunch of questions before shoving me in there."

"What did he want?" Hubbard prodded.

Castro paused. There was a line he was about to cross, and Hubbard needed him to come across it.

"Come on Gaspar," she urged. "I can't help you if you don't tell me everything."

"They'll kill me," he informed her. "I need protection. Witness protection or something."

She nodded, not agreeing to anything verbally. Not that any of that would matter. Hubbard could promise to move him to Italy to live out his life on a yacht in the Mediterranean. It wouldn't mean anything. But criminals were dumb, and she counted on that.

"Xavier took the girl," Castro confessed. "He's going to sell her, I think."

"Sell her?" Hubbard questioned. The idea repulsed her.

Castro wagged his head. "I heard the father torturing Lonzo until he told him where to go."

"Where is that?"

"Lonzo told him the church, but I think he'll take him out to the house down in the Glades."

"Why do you say that?" she questioned.

"Xavier will not keep the girl someplace the cops can find her. He's too smart for that."

His tone had the kind of admiration Hubbard had seen in domestic abuse situations. The praise felt forced, as if he was defending the man.

"Who beat the shit out of you?" she queried. "Was it Xavier?"

"I fucked up," Gaspar explained. "I shouldn't have taken the girl."

"Of course," Hubbard agreed. "You should have been smarter than that."

He let his head hang a little more.

"Where is this house?"

"I don't know," he said. "I've never been. Just heard some of the other guys talk about it. It's hidden down in the swamp somewhere."

Hubbard sighed. "What is the church?"

"It's the clubhouse," he explained. "Just an old church they converted to a clubhouse."

"Where is it?"

"Everglades City," he stated. "I don't know the address or nothing."

She nodded.

"The other man?" she asked. "You told him the same thing?"

Castro nodded.

"What did he look like?"

"Tall and blond. Looked like he was at the beach before he came here."

"The beach?"

"Yeah, he was wearing shorts and sandals. And a tank top."

"Really?" Hubbard clarified.

"His shirt was covered with blood and rips like a big fucking cat scratched him up."

Her brow furrowed. "He was injured."

Castro shrugged. "He didn't act injured. Just bloody."

She leaned back in the chair, her eyes drifted across the yard to land on Delp. Who the hell was this other guy? Another cop?

With her eyes on the detective, she pulled out her phone and texted Angie. Delp was connected to this other guy. Somehow Corsair was associated with both of them.

"Are you going to get me some protection?" Castro asked from the back.

"Yes," she lied. "You'll need to tell everything about killing the family and Xavier to one of the detectives, but I'll make sure they take care of you.

Gaspar Castro let out a sigh of relief.

Nineteen

Strangely, my arm didn't hurt. I mean, that's not entirely true. It did—both of them did. But where I deflected the ratchet didn't hurt as much as I expected, given I was dangling from a pair of handcuffs over a joist in the attic above the former church. It's possible that everything was hurting now. My body didn't have time to listen to my arm complain about how sore it was.

Caleb Saunders dangled across from me. When the members of *Las Serpientes* showed up, they took turns on us. Apparently, word made it back to the club about two dead bodies at their shop on Highway 41. The cops were all over the place. There must have been a call to regroup at their home base.

Caleb appeared to be unconscious, but I wasn't sure. I knew I'd been out for a small time, but I was more surprised they hadn't killed us yet.

"Caleb," I called to him. The man opened his eyes and stared at me.

"You okay?" I asked him.

"Yeah, five-by-five," he reported.

"Did you get anything from them?" I questioned.

"My guess is they plan to take us out into the swamp, shoot us, and drop us for the gators to feast on."

"That's good news," I responded.

"Seems hunky-dory to me," Caleb remarked. "What the hell are you doing here, anyway?"

This was the first time we were in the same room and someone wasn't shoving a gun in our respective faces.

"We showed up at the gas station about five minutes after you left in that old woman's car," I explained.

"We?"

"Jay Delp and I. Jay was with us at…"

Caleb nodded in recognition. "I remember. What was his call sign—Cotton? Right?"

"Yeah. Your memory is better than mine," I pointed out.

"Eidetic," he acknowledged.

"Handy," I stated before continuing, "I recognized you in the security footage."

"Why would you follow me?" he asked.

"You looked like you might end up in trouble," I suggested. "You were a Marine. We don't leave anyone behind."

"I was a Marine for seven seconds," he pointed out.

"A Marine's a Marine," I told him. "Besides, you were going after the people who kidnapped your daughter."

"I had it handled," he said bluntly.

"Obviously," I retorted, shaking my wrists. The motion dug the metal cuffs into my wrists, drawing blood. I felt the trickle as it ran down my arms.

"Do the police know my real name?" he asked.

"I'd say yes. Neither of us had your memory, so we only recalled your first name. However, there seem to be a couple of Homeland Security agents on the scene with a hard-on for you."

"The OOC," he explained. "The Office of Compliance. It's under Homeland, but only in name. It does the things the CIA and NSA find squeamish."

"Assassinations?"

"Among other things," he told me. "I dropped off their radar ten years ago. They might have assumed I was KIA, but I don't know. Now, I guess they know differently."

"Sorry," I apologized. "It's not like you left us a note."

"Doesn't matter," he mumbled.

"I don't suppose they are here to help you out of some dedication to their former employee," I commented.

"More likely they are here to make sure I don't resurrect myself again," he contradicted. "There are too many secrets I know the truth about."

"I'd guess by now they found the kid you left alive," I pointed out.

"What kid?"

"There was a guy behind the shop beat all to hell. I figured that was you."

"He's the one that shot Audrey," he remarked.

"Yeah, that was my guess."

"I wouldn't have left him alive," Caleb reported flatly.

"If they found him, it won't take long for him to give up this location. Jay was probably still with them, but I haven't talked to him since I left the shop."

"I need to get out of here," Caleb told me.

"I'm open to suggestions."

He pulled himself up and wrapped his fingers over the joist. Once he had his body weight in his own grip, Caleb twisted around so his back was to me.

"Can you kick off your sandals?" he questioned. "There's a lock pick set in my back pocket."

"They didn't take it?"

"No, the dumbasses took my gun, but didn't frisk me," he explained.

With the toe of the other foot, I pushed my right sandal off. After it fell about ten feet to the ground, I kicked the other one off and pulled up on the cuffs to get a grip on the wooden beam. My right foot swung toward Caleb's back pocket. Despite stretching, there was a twelve-inch gap between us.

"You need to scoot toward me," I ordered. "I can move about four inches before the cuffs are stopped by the truss."

He walked himself back by moving each hand over the other. With the cuffs restraining him, he couldn't move either hand very far. It was a slow process to cover about ten inches.

"Wait there," I told him. My foot stretched over, and my toes hooked on the back pocket.

It was an awkward position, and after about two minutes, I had to relax a few seconds before trying again. This time, I hooked my right foot around Caleb's legs to hold him still as I dug my toes into his pocket. The metal points scraped across the tip of my toe.

"Hang on," I warned. "I need to get in there deeper."

My right foot tugged his body closer as I shoved my toes into his pocket. The rip echoed in the attic as the stitches along one side popped.

"Don't lose it," he scolded.

"This isn't exactly the easiest thing to do," I snapped back, pushing my toes down.

My first two toes pinched the set.

"I think I got them. Let's do this slow."

He didn't respond. Instead, he seemed to stiffen so as not to move or sway. My foot pulled gently, dragging the lock picks out.

A ding froze me as I realized one pick slid out of my grip and clattered to the ground. I still had the sleeve that held them in between my toes, but I didn't know how many were still in it. Or if they were the right ones.

My feet balled up to clench them tightly once they were free. I released the grip my right foot had on Caleb, and the man swung away from me. Now I needed to get my foot up to my hand in a position I thought only a talented stripper could do. My arms pulled up. I felt the injured right arm lose its strength. The muscle in the left arm tensed as it held all my weight for several seconds until I could get my right arm to cooperate. Once I was steady, I swung my right foot up to hook it on the joist. Once that foot held a substantial amount of my weight, I carefully lifted my left foot up toward my head.

There was a time when I was in prime condition that I could do a kick that came up to my head. I was never as limber as some of those who specialized in those martial arts. I remembered a guy who could put his knee against his shoulder in a straight kick. The best I could do was put my toes within a foot of my face.

But that was standing on a mat. This time, I was short by almost two feet, and the momentum of my foot sent at least two picks out of the sleeve I was holding between my toes. My right hand closed around something that slapped against it. Then three distinct clinks sounded as the other three picks fell to the ground.

"Did you drop them?" Caleb gasped with some despair in his voice.

"I got one," I announced.

He let out a sigh of relief.

Now that the sleeve was empty, I let it fall from my toes. My left foot pulled up on the joist so I could use my right hand to pick the lock. It took me a few minutes, but the click as the cuff released itself was overly satisfying.

The next click we heard didn't elicit the same feeling. Someone was coming into the attic. I released my legs, holding the joist with my hands so I was hanging free.

"Wakey-wakey," a thick Latino announced. I hadn't seen him before. I guessed he was in his thirties. His face carried several scars that might have resulted from a knife or even a broken bottle. He had the look of someone who fought a lot. Not necessarily someone who won a lot of those fights, though.

"What do you want?" Caleb asked.

"The boss wants us to take you out for a little boat trip."

A second man walked through the door. I recognized him as the one who held the Mossberg twelve gauge on us earlier. It could have been the fact he was still holding the Mossberg loosely. He was more than thick. His denim jacket was tight around the arms, as if he'd gained some weight since he got it. Too proud to get a new one that actually fit. I bet he thought he was as tough as he used to be. It's possible—a Mossberg goes a long way to increase one's intimidation factor.

"A boat trip?" I quipped. "It's too late for one of those sunset cruises, isn't it?"

Knife Face dragged a six-foot painter's ladder over toward me. "We'll start with you, smartass," he informed me. The butt of the .357 he'd leveled at me earlier peeked out under his denim jacket.

"Yay for me," I remarked.

The man climbed up to the top of the ladder. Mossberg was standing back. His mistake was letting Knife Face put himself between me and the barrel of that shotgun. He still thought he was tough enough.

Knife Face reached to unlock the cuffs when I released the joist with my right arm. Thanks to physics, my body swung toward him when I let go. His eyes widened as I hit him in the face with my right fist. Once I let go with my left and wrapped it around him. My weight threw off his center of gravity, and the two of us fell off the ladder. The metal ladder flew out from under us with a crash.

Since I was on top of Knife Face, his body softened my impact. My arm was still wrapped around him, and I threw myself around, dragging him over on top of me. Normally, that wouldn't be ideal, but keeping something between me and the Mossberg was more important than giving Knife Face an upper hand.

Just to be safe, I punched my right hand into his throat. The punch hurt my hand, and it wasn't as effective as it should have been. However, if you can't hit hard, hit something vulnerable. The esophagus fits that bill.

He gasped audibly, stunned by the blow. My left hand reached for the .357 as I hit him again. I couldn't pull the barrel free of his holster, so I just squeezed the trigger. Over and over.

The sound a 357 makes is closer to a tank than most guns. At least when one is rolling around an enclosed space. The first round missed Mossberg, but he panicked and fired. Knife Face took the brunt of the round, ripping through the man. I felt my right arm burn as one pellet tore through my upper arm.

The second and third round from the .357 ripped into Mossberg's face. The man fell back through the door.

I pushed Knife Face's corpse off me, dragging the .357 free.

"Watch your face!" I shouted to Caleb as I aimed at him.

The Desert Eagle bucked, but I held it steady. It took three shots to sever the link between the cuffs.

Caleb dropped to the ground as the sound of footsteps clamored up the stairs behind Mossberg.

TWENTY

"His name is Chase Gordon," Angie explained over the phone. "He served in the Corps with Jay Delp. Currently, his address is listed at the Tilly Hotel and Marina in Palm Beach, Florida."

"The two are still friendly?" Lee Hubbard asked.

"Oh, yeah. This Gordon fellow pops up in all sorts of inquiries. There is even a DEA file open on him involving the death of an agent. Nothing seems to stick to him. It's safe to assume Delp keeps him clean."

"Is the guy dirty?" Hubbard questioned.

"Gordon? I don't think so. His military record is exemplary. Just like Delp's. They have more commendations than I have cats."

"That's a lot," Hubbard remarked mirthfully.

"Here's the kicker for you," Angie offered. "Gordon and Delp were in the same class at Parris Island as Saunders."

"No shit," Hubbard muttered. "I knew it."

"But there's no connection between the two of them and Thomas Harrod. Even after they left Parris Island, the three of them don't seem ever to be in the same place."

"At all?" Hubbard inquired.

"As far as I can tell," Angie replied. "I mean, I can't see the missions the OOC sent Saunders on, but the other two were mostly deployed with their Recon unit. Some of those missions have top secret classification, so unless those line up with something Saunders did, it doesn't track."

"It doesn't make sense," Hubbard admitted.

"Do you want my opinion?"

"Yeah, Ang," she answered.

"It's coincidence," Angie explained. "You said Delp looked like he was on vacation."

"Like he just got off a boat," she clarified.

"What if he was about to get on a boat?" Angie suggested. "Delp owns a fishing boat. Gordon has a sailboat. Both are registered in Florida. They could have been heading to the water and stumbled across the scene."

"That's a hell of a coincidence," Hubbard noted.

"Agreed," Angie confirmed. "I don't like coincidences, but they happen. Based on the shit this Gordon's gotten into since he's been out of the service, it looks like trouble follows him."

"You think they pulled into the gas station to find two murdered people and realize the victims' father and husband was an old Marine buddy? Based on that, they try to protect him?"

"You know some of those guys take the whole "Band of Brothers" thing to heart. Marines, especially. I dated a Marine several years ago. He kept driving across the country to drag an old buddy out of crack houses. Hell, Todd could have bought a new truck for the amount of money he spent trying to get that guy clean. It could be the same thing."

She continued, "Based on Gordon's military record, he defied an order to fly into a village in Afghanistan to rescue his commanding officer after her helicopter went down. That's the only blemish on his record. The officer who ordered him to stand down, a Colonel Wilson, tried to get Gordon for abandoning his post or some bullshit. His commanding officer had some pull higher up, and the whole affair now takes up an entire paragraph in his file."

"Great," Hubbard remarked. "He's an idealist. Delp is too. I could tell that from the start. He isn't going to go against his beliefs."

"Say what you will," Angie pointed out. "It's an attractive quality."

"Hmm," Hubbard groaned.

"Don't worry, I'm not chasing after any Marines," she promised.

Hubbard ignored the remark. "You have the address where the phone pinged last?"

"Everglades City. But it's not active anymore."

"Great," the agent muttered.

"Has Vickers given you any trouble yet?" Angie questioned.

"He's barely gotten out of the car," Hubbard told her. "Except the psychopath got an erection when we found the kid Saunders tortured. It was sick."

"I don't like it," the woman on the other end of the phone said. "You need to be ready to put him down if he turns on you. He's worse than a rabid dog."

"No kidding. At least the dog is foaming at the mouth. This bastard just stares at everything. I can't tell if he's even awake."

"Be careful," the woman urged again.

"I need to go," Hubbard announced before clicking off the line.

Jay Delp was standing next to the building across from the three bays converted into a garage. He gave the impression of a man trying to stay out of the way, but he remained attentive, like a neighbor trying not to appear nosy.

Arwoods and Cheney left to book Gaspar Castro, who was ready to blabber about everything, thinking he'd gotten a sweetheart deal. Hubbard hoped those two idiots didn't square Castro up to the fact there was no deal on the table.

Now that the coroner's office had picked up the bodies, the only people left on the scene were a couple of detectives and a crew of forensic crime scene specialists.

"What's the plan?" Delp questioned when he noticed her attention on him.

"You're going to tell me what you and Chase Gordon are up to," she informed him. "But you can do it in the car. I think we'll get his side of the story pretty soon."

"Did your friend on the phone tell you that already?"

"Let's go," she ordered. Jay Delp didn't move.

"What?" Hubbard asked with some frustration.

"I'm deciding if I want to go with you or not," he admitted. "I'm fairly certain your plans for Caleb Saunders are less than altruistic."

"Altruistic?" she repeated.

"Yeah," he responded. "It means doing something in the spirit of good."

"I know what it means, smartass," she snapped.

"Well, I'm from Mississippi," he explained. "It's never safe to assume the other person knows a five-dollar word."

Hubbard ignored his joke. "I don't give a rat's ass about Saunders or Gordon or you," she announced. "I have a job to do, and you're interfering."

"Technically, I'm not doing anything."

"Certainly not sharing information," she remarked. "Like the fact you and Saunders served together?"

"Well, we didn't," Delp corrected. "We were in basic together. That's it."

"It's something," she stated.

He nodded. "It is. But you haven't been overly forthcoming either," Delp suggested. "You don't carry around a torpedo like Vickers for his personality. Is he supposed to handle Saunders when you catch up to him? Is he too much for you to do? Or, I hope this is true: you have too many scruples to murder a man for no reason?"

Hubbard didn't answer for a second. Finally, she stated, "You can stay here. I'm going after your friend Gordon. Based on what I've seen in his file, he'll definitely get in the way of my 'torpedo.' Or you can help me get him out of the way so I can take Caleb Saunders into custody."

Delp shook his head with a bemused face. "I don't think Vickers is enough of a man to take out Gordon, and after seeing what Saunders has done, I'd say he has his work cut out for him there, too."

"You haven't seen the fucker work yet," Hubbard pointed out.

Delp turned his head to study the man leaning against the right front fender of the Lincoln Town Car.

"Okay, Agent Hubbard. Let's go," he offered. "I'd suggest you keep your pit bull leashed. We can solve this a lot easier without violence."

"I thought all Marines were ready to fight?" she questioned.

"There's a difference between being ready to fight and wanting to fight," he pointed out.

"What I saw in that garage makes it look like Saunders wants to fight," she mused.

"He might," Delp acknowledged. "But he's in a different mindset. There's a mixture of vengeance and despair there. He wasn't jonesing for a fight this morning. But now that it found him, he'll do what needs to be done. The same could be said of me or Chase. But I can take one look at your partner and see he wants to kill someone. That will end up getting him and, maybe you, killed."

Hubbard didn't respond as she approached the Lincoln. Instead, she ordered Vickers, "Get in. We're closing in on him."

Vickers grunted and moved to the front seat. He eyeballed Delp as the detective slid into the back seat.

"Where to then?" Delp asked.

"Everglades City," she stated as she started the car.

TWENTY-ONE

He stared at the silver plate mounted on the wall. The engraving along the edge resembled Mayan hieroglyphs. He didn't understand what they meant, and in fact, Xavier Jimenez suspected they meant nothing. The plate was one of the few things his mother had when she died. After going through her things, he didn't throw it out. The plate was pure silver, which meant it was worth something. He'd never had it appraised, but somehow it was comforting to see that money hanging on his wall.

After leaving the boathouse, Xavier motored east to his house in Chokoloskee, a little burg on the edge of the Ten Thousand Islands. He'd purchased a house on the canal with a boat dock. Technically, the house was still in his mother's maiden name. It was his own little oasis.

After handing the girl over to Angel, he wanted to get away from the club for a bit. The trip took a little longer than returning to Everglades City, but by the time he got here, he decided it was worth it.

The house was quiet when he entered. He flipped the seventy-inch television on, ignoring the sound but happy it killed the silence. He'd just dropped into the chair to find a ball game when Silva called.

"It's set," Silva told him. "Khaled will be there in the morning."

"That was quick," Xavier noted.

"He's coming back from Tampa," Silva explained. "It's on his way."

"How much?" Xavier wondered.

"He offered fifteen without blinking," Silva explained. "I told him twenty-five."

"Twenty-five? Damn."

"I didn't think he'd go as high as fifteen," Silva admitted. "But he jumped up there quick. I figured I'd shoot my wad."

"How's he paying?"

"Bitcoin."

"Good," Xavier replied. "You let Angel know the time. Deal?"

"Got it, man," Silva responded.

Xavier hung up the phone. *Las Serpientes* dealt flesh before, but most girls rarely got over ten thousand apiece. He assumed the Harrod girl's age played into the price. His stomach turned when he considered that, but this was business.

The phone rang again.

"Jefe, tenemos una problema," Antonio, one of Xavier's men, announced.

"What is it?" Xavier asked in English.

"The shop," Antonio explained. "Cops are all over it. Word is Ritchie, Gaspar, and the new kid are all dead."

"What the fuck?" Xavier exclaimed. "Who did it?"

"*No sé,*" the man told him.

"Where are you?" the leader asked.

"I'm over in Carnestown at Maria's," he answered.

Xavier took several seconds to think. He'd just been at the shop. Whoever it was could go after the club. Or they might be looking for the girl, he considered.

It made little sense. How would they have found the shop? The only thing he could imagine was the Mercedes had a tracking device. Ritchie would have disconnected it as soon as it got there, but that didn't mean someone didn't know where it was before the tracker stopped transmitting.

Besides, it would be the cops tracking the built-in GPS. They'd arrest everyone, not kill them. Ritchie would not make a stand against the cops, but Gaspar might. No, Xavier thought, Gaspar was too scared to go up against armed police. Lonzo was too smart to do that. It only made sense if someone else killed them.

"Antonio, get everyone you can back to the church. Something is going down."

"*Sí Jefe,*" the man responded before hanging up.

Xavier stared at the phone after Antonio disconnected. He put it on the table. The basketball game went into halftime, and a commercial for laundry detergent began declaring this product was the only one that could remove all the odors of sweat and grime after the kids come in from a game of football.

The man stood up and walked into the kitchen. In a drawer under the microwave, he removed another phone—an old flip phone variety. He dialed a number.

"Arwoods," the voice on the other end announced.

"What is going on?" Xavier asked flatly.

"Why are you calling me here?" Arwoods demanded in a heated voice.

"Watch your tone, Detective," Xavier warned. "Why are the cops all over my shop?"

"Fuck me," Arwoods mumbled. "Because your boys messed up."

"I pay you to steer the cops away from the club," Xavier pointed out. "Not let the whole department come down on my places of business."

"Listen, I couldn't do anything about that," Arwoods argued. "You got Feds down here. Apparently, the father of the family your guys killed is some kind of terrorist. This Agent Hubbard is going after him. He just happens to be going after you."

"How did they trace it back to the club?" Xavier questioned. "You need to control the investigation."

"It's not me," Arwoods continued. "The first person on the scene after your guys ran was an off-duty detective from Palm Beach County. Somehow, he tied it to *Las Serpientes* from the video footage."

"Shit," Xavier mumbled. Lonzo swore no one would identify them. "What happened at the shop?"

"Looks like the dad got there and killed your men. Left one guy alive. Gaspar Castro."

"Where's Gaspar?" Xavier asked.

"In custody at the Collier County Jail," Arwoods explained. "This has become a jurisdictional nightmare. Worse for you, though."

"What do you mean?"

"The Fed gave Gaspar the impression he'd get Witness Protection if he talked. The dumb bastard won't shut up now. He's already mentioned your name. I can't tell you how bad it will be if it gets out."

Xavier stewed. Gaspar was an idiot, but he could tie Xavier to a few things. Most importantly, the kidnapping of Amanda Harrod. He'd need to eliminate him before he caused any more damage.

"Where is this Fed now?"

"I left her at the storage place," Arwoods answered. "She knows where the church is, though. If she thinks this Harrod guy is heading there, she'll be right behind him."

"You need to shut Gaspar down," Xavier ordered.

"I don't know how you want me to do that," Arwoods retorted. "He's in holding in Collier County. I don't have any authority to go in there and do anything."

"You figure it out," he demanded, hanging up before he finished the sentence.

As he headed toward the garage, he stopped and pulled a nickel-plated Smith & Wesson forty-five. He'd left his other Harley at the shop, and for a second, he wondered if he'd get it back now. The eighty-seven model in the garage wasn't as comfortable, but it'd get him to the church. The engine rumbled to life, and Xavier pulled out of the drive heading toward Smallwood Drive, which took him north toward Everglades City.

TWENTY-TWO

When Caleb landed on the floor, he took two steps towards the door and grabbed the Mossberg shotgun dropped by the *Serpiente* I'd shot. After he'd retrieved the gun and stepped back from the door, he leveled it at the opening. His hand racked the sliding forearm back, expelling the spent shell. He'd have at most four rounds left in the Mossberg, assuming it was fully loaded.

I checked the .357—there were only three bullets left.

"What the hell's going on up there?" a voice shouted. Almost immediately, the guy at the bottom of the steps cried, "Juan's down!"

Caleb turned to look back at me. "We need to get out," he declared.

The attic space we were in was mostly unused. Exposed joists and plywood loomed over us. The floor was one-by-four planks running diagonally. A few stacks of boxes lined one side. The only light was a hanging bulb with a pull chain, and the light from downstairs stretched through the door, illuminating a trapezoid on the wood floor. On one wall there was a stained-glass window almost six feet from the peak, where the cupola and steeple rose from the roof.

"Pretty sure we have to go through them," I commented in a low voice.

"How many are down there?" he asked.

I shrugged. More than eight, which meant we were already outgunned.

"Make each shot count," he advised.

I reached up and pulled the chain on the bulb, extinguishing the light. Caleb and I stepped apart slowly, trying not to creak the wood under our feet. Eventually, someone had to come up to see what happened. Luckily, the stairwell and the door created a funnel. There was no way for them to rush us all at once. At best, they could come up two by two. We'd get four rounds of that before we were out of ammo.

On the plus side, they'd have eight bodies to climb over before anyone else made it into the room. Was this how the men in the Alamo felt? It seemed like an unfair comparison. After all, they had more ammunition.

It took several minutes before the stairs creaked as someone moved up them slowly. I couldn't see them, but the big man who'd had the shotgun slowly slid out of the doorway. As he vanished from sight, the clumping of his body as one of the bikers dragged it down the wooden steps echoed through the house.

Las Serpientes might have figured out a way to avoid climbing over the bodies. As I reflected, it occurred to me I should have stepped around the door and shot whoever was dragging the man down the stairs. On the other hand, that seemed foolish. Most likely there was a gun at the bottom of the steps covering them.

Caleb had vanished in the black shadows. I wondered how he'd be in a gunfight. His handiwork was on display at the chop shop, but he'd surprised them. Caleb made a good point, too. His stint as a Marine was nonexistent. How concerned was he going to be with covering my ass? Right now, his main concern was saving his daughter. Would he sacrifice me to do that?

I wished I'd called Jay before venturing in here. He'd find me, eventually. After all, I left Castro for him. He just had to get him to talk. How long would that take? The gang member might just lawyer up. By the time Jay got here, I might be feeding Wally Gator out in the swamp.

Caleb shuffled around in the dark. Something thumped to the floor.

"What are you doing?" I questioned in a whisper.

"Working on an exit strategy," he responded.

Any exit where I didn't get shot sounded like the start of a good plan. I didn't ask him what he had in mind. Instead, I waited.

Below us, movement indicated there was the potential for an uphill charge by the *Serpientes*. Someone down there might have been able to do the math. If Serpent One carried a 357 with nine rounds, and Serpent Two carried a Mossberg with five rounds. Even if they lost count or didn't know what we started with, it would make sense we didn't have enough firepower to gun them all down.

How they planned to choose the first ones to come up might prove to be an interesting sociological study. Maybe that was what took them so long to carry out the onslaught. Or whoever they appointed disagreed with the process. Whatever the cause, it was buying us time. For what, I hadn't figured out.

The best plan I had was to get one or two up the stairs, so when we shot them, we'd be able to grab their weapons. If the boys down below considered that, they might send the first wave up unarmed. That seemed like a bigger argument than just being picked to go first.

"Head on up there. We'll be right behind you."

"Can I have a gun?"

"No, they might take it off your corpse."

"Wait, what?"

"Get going."

I knew little about motorcycle gangs. The only thing I knew was none of these guys seemed as cool as Marlon Brando. Of course, I don't know if I'd be able to shoot Brando if I was facing him. It would be like gunning down Butch Cassidy or Billy Jack.

The sound of the Mossberg jacking a round out of the chamber echoed through the dark attic. It amazed me what ran through my head in times like this. For the moment, I was wondering if there was anything more iconic or recognizable than Brando's thoughtful intonation or the ejection of a shell from a twelve gauge.

The first round of volunteers came up the stairs with the trepidation that comes from a certain realization that each step might be the last one.

"You good?" Caleb asked from his corner. I took it to mean he was occupied and wouldn't be helping this time.

"Perfect," I lied, wondering how far I could let my first victim get before I dropped him.

The thought was slightly interrupted by the smell of gunpowder. It wasn't the familiar burnt powder odor. This reminded me of packing ammo.

A figure rushed through the door, and I stared down the barrel of the Magnum as a makeshift scarecrow made of a denim jacket and jeans stuffed with pillows filled the door before it fell forward on the floor.

"What the fuck?" Caleb muttered.

"Are you kidding me?" I shouted as I sprinted for the door. Whoever had been on the steps nearly fell as they scampered away from me.

"What the hell are you?" I blurted out. "Children?"

I suppose it was an insult to my intelligence. At least they could have attempted a better execution. Of course, had I fallen for the ruse, I'd feel pretty shitty right about now. Better to gloat.

Loud footsteps clumped onto the steps. My eyes remained glued to the door.

"*Amigos*, this is foolish," a deep voice boomed up the steps. "You have nowhere to go, and you are severely outgunned."

"Then come on up here," I called back.

"Eventually I will," he remarked. "I don't particularly want to put bullet holes through my club, but if we don't come to an agreement, I recently got an M4 that I've been dying to use."

The voice chuckled. "Ah," he added. "Irony. You'll be dying if I use it."

"Good luck," I retorted. "You'll get a full second to fire that bitch before I put a round between your eyes."

He laughed. "*¡Eres valiente!*"

It sounded like Caleb laughed under his breath. I hoped he had a plan formulating. So far, all I'd heard him do was shuffle paper and overturn boxes. If *Las Serpientes* kept their Christmas grenades up here, we might have a chance.

Caleb straightened up and walked to the center of the attic. I watched him from the corner of my right eye while my left stayed locked on the stairwell. The man unscrewed the light bulb and set it on the ground. He reached up with his fingers and pried at the ceramic light fixture nailed to the wooden joist. After a few seconds, he pulled the nails out of the wood. His fingers rocked the fixture back and forth, pulling it away from the rafter.

Once it was free, Caleb grabbed the white cable running from the light down to the electrical panel. Small U-shaped fasteners held the cable up along the rafter, but when he yanked on the wire, the small nails securing the fasteners popped out with ease. He dragged the excess wire back into the dark.

"That's it," the voice downstairs announced. "You're done."

A burst of gunfire splintered the wooden frame at the top of the door. I stepped back from the entrance. There was no way to know which way he'd shoot first, but despite what I threatened, there wasn't a lot three rounds would do against an M4 with a thirty-round magazine.

A pop in the corner illuminated the darkness for a split second. Then it happened again, and I realized Caleb was creating the spark by touching the positive and negative wires running through the cable. The third spark flamed up with a sizzle that sounded through the room just as another four rounds from the M4 ripped into the wood near the door. The gunman was hoping to push us back as he and likely a few others came up the stairs.

A second later, the flame on the other side of the room flared up as the old cardboard and papers fed it. The tongues of fire jumped up against the wood wall.

"Shit," I muttered as the fire found the old wood in the church delicious. Caleb's plan was to burn us out. It occurred to me I was wrong. There were escape plans that didn't involve me getting shot I wasn't too keen on.

Shadows filled the door way as the *Serpientes* pushed forward. Smoke filled the attic, and I dropped to the floor. The .357 bucked in my hands once as I put a single round just inches from the shadow. It was a wasted shot, but it slowed the motorcycle gang's ascent.

"*¡Fuego!*" someone in the stairwell screamed.

"*¡Mierda!*" the deep voice cursed as a figure stepped into the light.

The muzzle of the M4 flashed as he sprayed bullets over my prostrate body. I squeezed the trigger, firing the .357. The man in the door way jerked and fell back. Caleb took three fast strides toward the fallen form. Through the smoke, I watched him raise the shotgun in his hand as he threw himself across the opening. The boom reverberated through the room. I watched the smoke billow away from the barrel as the force of the shot displaced the air.

My ears rang, leaving me unable to tell if anyone else was charging up the stairs. The flames were crawling up the wall now, and the entire attic space flickered in a bright orange.

Caleb picked up the M4, cradling it against his shoulder. The Mossberg fell to the floor, and he stood at the top of the stairs pointing the M4 down. If anyone came up the stairs, he could mow them down.

I crawled under the layer of smoke, which was quickly filling the attic. Staying up here would only kill us now. Caleb and I faced a reversed situation from the bikers earlier. We were now about to climb out of the funnel. But at least we were better armed now.

"Nice shot," he commended me when I rose beside him.

"I warned him," I pointed out, reaching over the man as I grabbed the Mossberg. The lifeless face stared up at me, and I noticed the braided beard. It looked ridiculous.

The Magnum was down to one shot. There should have been three shells in the shotgun if Caleb only used the gunpowder from one to start the fire. I slipped the .357 under my waistband and raised the shotgun.

"We need to move," Caleb announced. "I'll take the lead."

The man moved like he'd been born a soldier. I couldn't believe he hadn't ever made it to active duty. Every move was fluid as he eased down the steps.

At that point, a shot rang outside the church. Then another. As we reached the bottom of the stairs, the windows of the church exploded in gunfire.

TWENTY-THREE

A t first, the pair waited. Until the gunfire started. Something was happening. Men in leather and denim ran around in a frantic state.

The two men stood in different windows of the single-story Spanish ranch house down the street. In the bathroom just off the living room, two bodies belonging to the owners of the house had been stacked in the aqua-green porcelain tub. They sliced both of their throats open. Their only mistake was opening the door when the bell rang.

Jacob and Walter might have been brothers. They weren't. At least, the consensus seemed to be that they weren't. Although the consensus remained almost nonexistent. Jacob and Walter didn't talk to many people. The best others might do is guess.

In public, they seemed like acquaintances. They never smiled. No secretive glances. No private jokes.

The people who came in contact with the two avoided those personal questions. Some thought the men looked alike enough to be related. Both had the same olive-tinted skin and round brown eyes. Even their gaunt facial features looked the same.

If you dropped them in most cities in the United States, they'd blend into the population on contact. One of their few business associates remarked to another that the two men seemed not only interchangeable but utterly forgettable.

Whatever the story behind Jacob and Walter, the only truth people knew was they were two of the deadliest killers on the East Coast. When word came through the network they depended upon for work, it seemed like an opportunity. Find the man known as Corsair and deliver him to Manhoud Abbas in Qatar, and receive a reward of twenty million pounds. An ungodly payout for one man.

Tracking a man who'd been a ghost for a decade would usually prove difficult. Except Walter had a contact inside Carl Winston's office. Winston's agents closed in on Corsair. Their contact gave them a head start, and the two men arrived thirty minutes ago.

Now they watched as something happened inside the old church. The gun shots sent both men into action. Walter opened two identical cases and removed the two matching H&K G36s. He snapped a C-mag into each assault rifle while Jacob slipped what looked like a black leather jacket, designed especially for Jacob over his toned shoulders. Walter had an identical one. Each coat had a layer of Kevlar sewn into the liner. Two holsters holding Glock

19s hung on the inside of each lapel, along with a pocket for an extra magazine and a sheath for a small blade with a hand-carved bone handle.

Walter handed one G36 to Jacob before donning his jacket. Jacob checked the rifle before allowing the stock to rest in his left hand. Each man reached inside his respective cases and removed a set of four-eye tactical night vision goggles. The straps stretched over their heads, and the ocular lenses raised. Without a word between them, Walter and Jacob moved outside of the house in unison.

Outside, the men separated, lowering their lenses. The landscape glowed green. Red and orange figures scurried around. Jacob moved to the east side of the church. The church glowed, and the air around it swirled with hints of red.

One biker pointed in his direction. He heard the man shout something. The biker didn't get his words out before the first forty-five-millimeter round from Jacob's gun burrowed in the man's skull. Another biker fired wildly in the dark.

Through the windows of the building, Jacob watched two figures descending a flight of stairs. The two men moved slower than the rest. He lifted the G36 to peer down the sight.

He squeezed the trigger, firing in bursts of eight. The sound of breaking glass bounced between the church and the other houses. Two of the gang members came around the back of the church. Jacob pivoted on his right foot and squeezed the trigger. Two rounds hit each man in the chest. By the time their bodies hit the ground, he'd turned to fire into the church again.

The two figures weren't visible, but he didn't think he'd hit them. With too many obstacles inside the building, he couldn't find them.

He strode toward the church, twisting after three steps to shoot a man charging him. His gaze shifted for half a second to see the roof of the church flickering as small flames ate through the top. The fire was climbing up, and within minutes it would run out of roof to climb. After that, it would devour the church to the ground.

In his head, he assumed the response time would be about twenty minutes. The only fire department in the area was a volunteer one, and with only three police on duty, it wasn't likely a minimum wage cop thought it wise to charge into a veritable war zone. They'd be waiting for someone with a higher rank to make those decisions. Jacob guessed that the guy had been home for a couple of hours. Right now was when he was getting the call that there was a disturbance. Since *Las Serpientes* weren't new to town, they might not rush to their defense either.

He stepped onto the front steps, firing at a group of bikers huddling behind a line of motorcycles. If Jacob smiled, he might have done so, then as twenty rounds pinged and punched through those bikes. A small whoomp sounded as one of the Harley's fuel tanks caught fire. The leaking fuel tanks from the other bikes fed the starving fire, and in a second, the six bikes were all aflame.

Jacob pushed through the door. The building had cleared out. There were at least a couple of *Serpientes* still floating around, and Jacob was ready to finish them before they did anything.

He scanned the floor for bodies. The inside of the church felt like a sauna, only the air was filled with soot and smoke swirling about.

Corsair hadn't run out the front, but if he went out the back, Walter was there to stop him.

Jacob moved through the house. The downstairs was empty. Fire was pouring down the steps. It was only minutes before the rafters above him crumbled. He stepped through the kitchen to see the rear door open. When he walked out on the back deck, he saw a figure face down on the gravel yard. The man wore the same leather jacket as Jacob.

The killer dropped his G36 and rushed to the figure, rolling it over to see Walter's lifeless face. A hand-carved bone handle protruded from his eye. His neck gaped open from a single gunshot.

TWENTY-FOUR

"Where's this boathouse?" Caleb demanded, pressing the barrel of the M4 into the Latino biker's throat.

The man quivered on the ground. I couldn't blame him. He'd just watch Caleb disarm the pale man in the leather jacket and drive the man's own knife into his eye.

After the windows of the church shattered around us, we took cover behind the bar for a second. Caleb didn't pause long, except to decipher our best exit. I'd been in lots of firefights, and I consider myself skilled in my ability to analyze the situation and find the best solution. But Caleb seemed to work on an infinitely faster scale. No sooner had we hit the wood floor, the spy moved across the room with intent. I followed him as he barrel-rolled through a shattered window.

It surprised the man shooting up the church when Caleb crashed out of the church and landed almost on top of him. The shooter fired an H&K G36 with a drum magazine. I'd seen several Rangers carrying those overseas. With the drum, he could have a hundred rounds.

However, Caleb raised up from the ground as the man lifted the G36. He caught the barrel with his bare hand and wrenched it free in a swift motion. The eyes on the shooter widened when he realized Caleb had never flinched at the hot barrel. It took him a split second to recover from the shock and whip out a five-inch dagger with a carved bone handle. The man swiped the blade toward Caleb, who stepped into the man's swing. He caught the guy's wrist with his left hand. He twisted and slammed his right elbow into the man's face. Before I knew what happened, the knife was in Caleb's grip as he drove it into the man's face.

The man fell back on the ground, and Caleb shifted his gaze toward the carnage around us. A biker stared at us after coming around the corner. His eyes shifted behind us as the man with the knife in his eyeball pushed up off the ground, reaching under his coat again.

I fired the last round in the .357 at him. His head snapped back as the bullet ripped through the man's esophagus and exited out the base of his skull, shattering the occipital bone.

"Stay down!" I demanded as Caleb fired the M4 at the biker, hitting him in the knee.

The *Serpiente* dropped, screaming and grasping at his leg. Caleb took four steps toward the man and kicked him in the chest.

"Where's the girl?" he demanded.

"My leg!" he howled. "You shot my knee!"

Caleb lowered the M4's barrel to the man's other knee. "Do you want to lose the other one?"

"No, man," the biker pleaded. "No!"

"Where is the girl?" he repeated. Caleb didn't call her by her name or even refer to her as his daughter. He was treating her like a target. How dispassionate was he really? I picked up the G36 and stepped up behind him, covering his six.

"I don't know, man," he responded, tears streaming down his face. He had to be wondering if he was about to die. "I heard Xavier took her to the boathouse."

"Where's the fucking boathouse?" he demanded.

The biker stared up at him without answering.

Caleb pressed the M4 against the man's throat. "Where's this boathouse?"

He shook, answering, "Out in the Glades."

"How do I get there?"

The biker shook his head. "I can't remember. I have it in my GPS."

"Give it to me," Caleb ordered.

"No, man," he insisted. "The chart plotter on my boat."

Caleb glanced back at me. I nodded, indicating I was here for the entire ride. He reached over and caught the man by his stringy black hair, dragging him to his feet. "Where's your boat?"

"Across the road," he bellowed, wincing in agony.

"Let's go," he commanded.

The biker took a step and collapsed under the ruined knee.

"He'll slow us down," I pointed out.

Caleb turned and looked at him. He shrugged, raised the M4, and fired a single shot. *Las Serpientes* was down another man. There could be an argument for why Caleb should have left him alive. He would not come after us, but that wouldn't stop him from telling others. I don't know if I'd have shot him, but then my daughter's life wasn't in the balance. To me, this was war. Caleb didn't start it, but he'd decided already to finish it. By the time the day was done, I imagine the surviving *Las Serpientes* members would regret crossing paths with the Harrod family.

I followed Caleb as he crossed behind the burning church. We crossed the small road I'd driven down earlier when I was running recon on the church. Caleb seemed to know where he was going as he stepped off the street into the grass growing up. Even in the dark, I made out the well-worn path through the brush. When we reached the water's edge, there was a floating dock with three boats tied to it—an airboat, an older pontoon, and a fishing boat. The airboat and the pontoon had a chart plotter attached to the helm.

"Which one?" I asked.

"Pontoon," he remarked. "That bastard's hair would get sucked into the blades."

He climbed aboard and pulled the ignition out of the old helm. It was easy. The wood used to construct the helm was soft from years of sitting on the water. The vinyl upholstery ripped as the round keyhole tore free. Caleb ripped the red and black wire from the back of the ignition and wound them together. The screen on the GPS lighted, casting a white glow on Caleb's face.

He stared, somewhat dumbfounded, at the helm.

I reached over his hand and pressed a button next to the fuel gauge. The twenty-horsepower Nissan outboard turned over three times before the engine spat and rumbled.

"Damn," he whispered. "I missed it."

"I've been on my fair share of boats," I remarked.

"Do you know how to use the GPS?" he questioned.

"Let me in there," I told him, and he stepped away from the helm. He cradled the M4, watching the brush behind us for any intruders.

I tapped on the commands on the menu screen until I found the saved routes. There were three. I backed out of that section and found the history. There were several quick trips to various places only a few miles from here, but there were seven trips that covered about forty to fifty miles. It was hard to judge the distance with all the jack leg turns and winding channels.

"I think this might be it," I told Caleb.

"You sure?"

I shook my head. "No, they didn't label it, but it seems the farthest out of the way."

"Let's go," he told me.

"Untie those lines," I ordered, pointing to the bow and stern lines securing us to the dock. He hurried to the front and the back, pulling each line aboard.

I pressed the throttle forward, easing us away from the platform. Mounted on the top of the awning was a spotlight. I wanted to get away from the dock before we lit up the swamp. No point in making us a target.

That meant I was relying solely on the GPS for the next few minutes. I'd pulled into a few anchorages in the dark, but this was different. The water in the Everglades is notoriously shallow and full of logs, fallen trees, mangroves, and who knows what else. Also, I wasn't familiar with it. All of that meant that I was taking it very slowly as I held the small arrow representing the pontoon boat tightly on the highlighted course.

After a few minutes, we motored out of the clearing. Even in the dark, I could see the trees closing in as we entered the channel. I worked to keep the boat in the middle of the canal. I figured we were far enough from the dock to risk the light. The switch was on the stern facing side of the helm, and when I flipped it up, the LED lights flashed on illuminating the 180 degrees in front of the boat.

"Is that an alligator?" Caleb asked, staring ahead.

My eyes followed his to see two glowing eyes just above the surface.

"Sure is," I answered.

"Jackson, we made it," he whispered in a throaty tone.

I didn't turn my head from him.

"I'm sorry," he continued.

He wasn't talking to me.

"Sorry, Chase," he interjected. "We were coming to the Everglades this morning. Jackson was so excited to see the alligators."

He sucked in a breath. I didn't respond.

"I was worried we would not see one. You know how it can be. We drove through the Smoky Mountains looking for bears and saw none. I didn't want him disappointed."

"You'd probably have had no trouble seeing them," I told him.

"I was worried he wouldn't see an alligator," he mused. His voice cracked. "I didn't think he'd never make it."

"I don't have to tell you it wasn't your fault," I offered.

He cleared his throat. "No, it wasn't. Maybe it was. I got complacent."

"You were on vacation," I pointed out. "This wasn't Iraq or Afghanistan. It was a family vacation."

"You know, I should have known better than to expect a normal life," he remarked, wiping away a tear I couldn't see. "I did too many things to deserve that."

"Not true," I corrected. "You aren't the only one who's done those things. What we did was for a reason."

He shook his head. "No, what you did was with purpose. At first, I thought I was doing what was needed to protect my country. After a while, I knew that wasn't the case. Even when

I realized I wasn't working for America, I didn't stop."

I pressed the throttle down to speed up the pontoon now that I could see the water ahead of me.

Caleb continued, "I think I liked it."

I shrugged. "I liked it," I remarked. "Not like a psychopath, but there's a feeling that comes after battle as the adrenaline is rushing out. You feel alive again. Like right now—we just escaped a group of armed combatants.

"That's why I walked away when the time came," I added. "You walked away too. That means something."

He nodded.

The course on the chart plotter told me to veer to port and follow a small opening in the mangroves. The pontoon's awning scraped the mangrove branches as we passed through the path.

"It was a kid," Caleb commented.

I glanced over my shoulder at him.

"I went into a building in Alexandria. The target was in an apartment there. The file I'd received said he was the leader of an Al-Qaeda cell. I was supposed to set off a small explosive—make it look like they accidentally blew themselves up. The device I had malfunctioned, and I opted for Plan B, you know? When I got into the apartment, I found a mother and her nine-year-old boy. They had no affiliation with any terrorists. The boy's father worked for a tech company that supplied computer chips for targeting sensors. The mission was supposed to eliminate his family and label him as a terrorist. Simply to cover that the design was stolen."

"What did you do?" I asked.

"I blew up the apartment after all," he told me. When I stared at him blankly, he added, "The family was gone. I helped them escape, and I faked my death."

"Wouldn't they have looked for a body?"

He nodded. "I provided one. The security chief for the tech firm. He was behind a few other deaths, and he tried to kill the family when it seemed like I had failed. I let him come to take care of the job, and I finished it instead."

"What are you going to do now?" I asked.

"Doesn't matter," he commented. "If I don't get Amanda back, nothing matters."

TWENTY-FIVE

When the Lincoln pulled onto the street, Hubbard gasped at the carnage in front of her. Flames jumped from a building in front of her. Fire consumed the entire structure, so that even the steeple appeared to be a flaming spire. Smoke filled the streets like a heavy black fog, and the stench of burning wood permeated the car. There were a few men standing back from the fire, watching with expressions of both revulsion and awe.

"What the hell?" Hubbard muttered. "What happened?"

She glanced at Delp, who stared at the flames with an odd smirk of satisfaction. Lee Hubbard didn't need to be a mind reader to understand his thoughts. He was sure that this resulted from Corsair or Chase Gordon. Possibly both.

Vickers's head turned away as they approached the burning church.

Hubbard grabbed her phone and dialed 911.

The operator answered, "What is your emergency?"

"This is Agent Hubbard with Homeland Security. We have a structural fire at," Hubbard paused, scanning the street for a sign. "Collier and Datura," she read into the phone. "There are armed men on the premises. We'll need police support."

She hung up and pulled her Kel Tec PF-9. "Let's contain this and find Saunders," she ordered Vickers before looking to Delp to demand, "You stay here."

The other man didn't respond, and Hubbard exited the vehicle raising her firearm as she approached the crowd. Delp climbed out of the back seat, ignoring her order. Vickers also got out of the car, but he turned and walked away from the burning building.

"Homeland Security!" Hubbard shouted at a cluster of *Las Serpientes* watching their club burn. The men turned to see the armed agent approaching.

"*¡Corre!*" one of them shouted, and the group split up, running in different directions.

Hubbard didn't give chase—she wasn't interested in any of them. As long as they weren't resisting or interfering, she wasn't concerned. Her head swiveled to find Vickers no longer there.

"Dammit," she cursed the man who was supposed to be her backup.

"I got your six," Delp alerted her, stepping up behind her.

"I told you to stay with the car," she scolded.

"You also told Vickers to follow you," he pointed out. "I guess neither of us is good at listening."

"Where did he go?" she asked.

The detective shrugged. "Can't get good help," he remarked.

"You stay right with me," she ordered. "If you interfere with my apprehension of Saunders, I'll make sure you never see the light of day."

He lifted his hands—a symbol of surrendering agreement. "I just don't want to see you shot in the back," he advised. "That would be a damned shame, if you ask me."

Hubbard stared at the man. "Are you flirting with me?" she asked.

"I've been flirting with you all day," he remarked, bringing a stupid, sheepish grin to Hubbard's face.

"Well, stop it," she warned. "I don't have time for that."

"Not sure how much time you need to be flirted with," he commented.

The agent ignored him. "Stay with me," she repeated.

Delp nodded, and the agent moved toward the burning structure.

Neighbors stood on their porches, filming the flames with their cell phones. A loud crack echoed through the neighborhood as the back section of the roof collapsed. Sparks exploded up into the dark sky like swarms of fireflies.

"Don't get too close," Delp warned. "Anything in there is literally toast."

"You think Saunders is here?" she questioned.

"I'd guess he was here," he answered.

"You think he's gone by now?"

"I see it like this," he explained. "Either he was inside the church, in which case he's dead. Or he caused this, in which case he's gone already."

"Where would he go?"

"He came here for his daughter," Delp said. "If she was here and alive, he left with her. If she wasn't here, he is going after her."

"He'll be off the grid soon."

Delp nodded as they marched a wide path around the back of the building.

"I don't think he was in the building, if that makes you feel better," Delp stated, as he pointed at the pale corpse lying on the dirt with a knife sticking out of his eye.

Hubbard's face curled in disgust. "Who is he?" she asked. "He doesn't dress like one of the biker gang."

Delp knelt down next to the body. "This is an expensive flak jacket. Custom made."

"A hitter?" she questioned.

"He certainly doesn't fit the demographic for *Las Serpientes*," he added.

"How did he beat us here?" she wondered aloud.

"Probably the same way you did," Delp pointed out.

"I got my information from a trusted source," she assured him.

"Hmm," he mused.

"What?"

"Where did your source get their info?" he pondered.

"Damn," she cursed.

"If you're tracking Chase's phone, which I assume you've been doing, then all they had to do is give this guy the information before they gave it to your source," he explained. "A half hour head start can give them plenty of time."

Delp cocked his head, staring at the corpse. "Not that half an hour did him a lot of good."

Hubbard let her shoulders slump. Delp watched her for a minute before straightening up and staring down the street.

The agent noticed his eyes shifting in a far-off gaze. "What is it?" she asked.

"My Jeep," he responded, pointing about a block east at the Jeep and boat parked on the side of the road.

Hubbard perked up. "Does that mean Gordon is here?"

Another crash behind them pulled their attention around as the steeple toppled back. As it struck the remaining roof, the wooden rafters cracked, sending embers blowing out in a cloud of sparks. Delp stared at the collapsing building.

"You think he was in there?" she asked.

"I hope not," he answered.

Hubbard grabbed his arm, forcing him to turn his eyes toward her. "You can't assume he is," she advised. "It makes sense if Gordon is with Saunders. We know he got out."

Delp glanced back at the body on the ground. His eyes moved about 150 feet away from where another body sprawled on the ground. He walked over to examine the biker. The man had been shot in the right knee and the chest. He stared at the body as Hubbard walked over.

"That's not him," she pointed out.

"No, but here," he said, his finger traced through the air. "Right there. It's blood spray. Then, a short blood trail to here."

"Yeah, so?"

"From the splatter on the ground, I'd say he was facing the other direction. Like he was looking directly at our hitter over there when someone shot his knee out. He stood up and walked about eight to ten feet before he was shot in the chest. Plus, there's this smear of blood on the man's pants. It's a hand print. Smeared, but I can make out the fingers."

Hubbard stared at the dried blood. "I don't get it."

"Chase didn't do this," he told her. "If he shot him in the knee, it was because this guy didn't have a gun, or at least wasn't threatening him. It would just incapacitate him. I don't know Saunders, but I think he shot the guy in the knee. He wants to find his daughter. I think this guy told him where to go, but he couldn't make it."

"And Saunders killed him? Unarmed?"

Delp pointed out, "He blames them for killing his family and kidnapping his daughter. Death and destruction seem to be his calling card."

He stood up and waved at the church as the side wall nearest them collapsed. "He might have gotten the girl's location out of him before he died. Offered him some first aid for the information, and once he got it, he wiped his hands clean of the man."

"Good observation," she noted. "That's cold, though."

He shrugged as if Hubbard expected it.

"How do we find the girl?" she asked.

Delp stared back at the Lincoln. "Where did Vickers go, really?"

"I don't know. He's a psychopath," she remarked. "He doesn't want to do anything I say."

"Sociopath," he corrected. "But he's been just hanging around waiting. Now he isn't. Where did he go?"

Hubbard scanned the area. She'd been dreading the moment when Vickers went off-book. What was his motivation? Like Angie warned, she'd assumed from the moment Carl Winston assigned Vickers that there was an ulterior motive.

Honestly, Hubbard considered if Vickers only ventured off on his own. At least she didn't have to worry about him turning on her.

"Come on," she urged Delp. "I need to regroup."

He followed her to the black Lincoln. All the bikers vanished after Hubbard announced she was with Homeland. The only people out were the neighbors still watching the burning pile of embers that had once been a church.

Where were the local cops? Hubbard wondered. Or the fire department? This city wasn't big, but they had to at least have a volunteer fire department.

Maybe the bikers had enough of a reputation that everyone ignored calls to their club. A fire might resolve a pest problem the town had been dealing with.

"Detective," she called to Delp.

Delp leaned against the car next to her.

"I'm at a loss," she muttered. "Saunders may have won."

"Somehow, I doubt he sees today as a win for him," Delp remarked. He stared off into the darkness, thoughtful.

"When we pulled up, Vickers saw something," he suggested.

"What do you mean?" she asked. "What was it?"

He shrugged. "I don't know. It didn't register with me. Most of us look around in the car, but Vickers stared ahead the whole time. He'd check on me in the back seat, but he'd only flick his eyes up in the mirror when he thought I wasn't watching."

"But?"

"He turned his head when we pulled up. As if he'd seen something requiring a double take."

Delp pushed off the car and walked toward the road. Brush grew up over the other side of the street. He crossed into the brush and waded through the grass. He smelled the water.

Hubbard pushed through the weeds behind him. "What are you looking for?"

He stopped and pointed fifty feet west of them, where a dock floated. Secured to the platform was an old bass boat.

"You think Vickers took a boat?" she asked.

The surface of the water was still rolling with small waves created when a boat passed over it. The ripples would bounce back and forth off the shore for a few moments before the water turned still again.

He turned to look at her. "I think they all did."

"The boathouse Castro told me about."

"What boathouse?" Delp asked.

"He said Xavier probably took the girl to a house in the Everglades."

"A house?"

"Boathouse."

He turned at stared over the surface of the water.

"Let's go," she urged.

"Unless you know where you're going, that will not do us a lot of good. There are over seven thousand square miles of glades out there. We'd be searching forever."

"How would Vickers know where to go?" she asked.

"You'll have to ask your partner that," he suggested.

She let out a sigh.

"Let me make a call," he offered, stepping back out of the brush to stand on the street.

Hubbard stood on the shore of the lake. An eerie feeling came over her. She'd never been to the Everglades before. Her idea of the area was that it was nothing but swampland filled with snakes, alligators, and a few bears.

Five minutes passed before Delp returned.

"Who did you call?" she asked.

"A ranger," he answered. "He's over at the Welcome Center. Here's the thing. There are about ten to fifteen shacks built out there. Even more blinds and sheds. But he said there are two on this side of the Glades. There are a couple of folks living out there, but they probably think they're hiding. The rangers might not check them regularly, but they know about every man-made structure out there."

"Can we go?" she asked.

"Here's the kicker, though. Both are about forty miles away, but they're in two different directions."

"Damn," she muttered. "Where are they?"

"He's going to ping me the coordinates. We just have to decide which one to go to. We'd never be able to do both. If we choose wrong, by the time we get back to the other, it'll be too late."

She started toward the bass boat.

"Wait." Delp grabbed her arm. "We have to wait for him to send the coordinates. Let's get my boat."

Twenty-Six

After a few seconds on the ground grieving the fallen Walter, Jacob bounded to his feet. Rage flooded his body, washing away grief and greed. He wanted Corsair to die in his grasp. The contract by Abbas could be damned. He now had his own score to settle, and the money made no difference to him.

Jacob found the wheezing biker close to Walter's body. The man obviously crossed paths with Corsair. The first shot obliterated his right knee, and the sucking wound in his chest would kill him soon.

"Where did he go?" Jacob demanded, kneeling over the figure.

"The girl," the biker struggled to say.

The man's daughter was missing still. When Jacob and Walter reached out to their source in the Office of Compliance, they confirmed the details. Corsair was still looking for the girl. That would be his demise, Jacob thought. Funny how stupid sentimentality would lead a world-class assassin to his death, he mused.

"Where is she?" he asked, trying to press his hands against the wound to slow the man's dying.

"The boathouse," the biker coughed. "In the Glades."

"Where?" Jacob questioned.

The man's last movement was a barely perceptible shake of his head. Jacob wiped his bloodied hands on the man's jeans.

If the girl was in a boathouse, it would be on the water. He removed his phone from his jacket and pulled up a satellite image of the area. There was a lake just across the street that tied to the Everglades. That would be the direction Corsair would go, Jacob decided.

He paused for a moment, glancing back at the fallen figure of Walter. Then he marched toward the street. There were still a few bikers scurrying around. They didn't know what to do except watch the building burn. He held the G36 ready to kill any that came his direction, but they all seemed to only watch him as he walked away. These weren't the high-level club members, he figured. Those were the ones who came after him early on. Jacob killed them. The rest learned enough to stay back for now.

He chuckled to himself, supposing that now they were all promoted thanks to him.

On the phone screen, he zoomed in closer to this area. There was a dock with boats tied to it in the image. If he hurried, he might catch Corsair there as he headed out onto the water. He walked through the grass toward the pier.

In the distance, the rumble of a motor rolled across the water. With the trees and the water distorting the noise, he couldn't distinguish how far it was. If he hurried, he'd be able to catch him.

Jacob stared at the airboat tied up to the dock. The other two options were small fishing boats. He knew little about boats. While he'd driven a few, those were limited to wide open lakes in the daytime. The airboat seemed like the best choice. It was a swamp, and the fishermen out here used these boats for a reason. It took him a few minutes to fire the motor up.

Shit, he cursed. He needed to untie the boat. The G36 leaned against the raised seat, and Jacob moved along the edge of the boat untying the line at the bow. He heard the footsteps on the wood pier. He pulled the Glock 19 from under his jacket.

"Put it away," a voice told him.

He held the nine-millimeter up and flipped the night vision goggles down. The tall figure eased out onto the dock, and Jacob leveled the weapon at him.

"I said, 'Put it away,' Jacob," he repeated.

Jacob paused, recognizing the voice. "What are you doing here?" he asked the man who'd provided the information to him.

"Trying to manage the situation," Vickers explained. "Where's Walter?"

Jacob's head drooped. "Dead."

"Corsair?" Vickers questioned.

He nodded.

"They escaped into the swamp?"

"I believe so," Jacob affirmed. "They are looking for the daughter."

"She's being held in a boathouse somewhere out there," Vickers explained. "That's what Hubbard found out."

"I heard a boat," Jacob explained.

Vickers stepped into the airboat. He took a second to survey the controls. The throttle was a handle next to the raised seat. Another handle adjusted the flaps on the large prop cage. Simple design, but he suspected it took some skill and expertise to operate it well.

There was a GPS plotter attached to the helm as well. He keyed up the screen until he found the map. He followed similar keystrokes as Chase did until he found the history as well. There were several trips, but only one route seemed to be far enough out of the way and repeated enough to be the one they were looking for.

"Untie us," Vickers ordered.

"I'm going to kill him," Jacob told the man. "For what he did to Walter."

"Jacob, you're being foolish," Vickers advised. "He'll die, but let's get paid for it."

"It's not fair," the other man blurted out.

"No," Vickers corrected him. "You want him to suffer. That's easy enough. Find the girl and force Corsair to watch as you kill her slowly."

Jacob's mouth turned up in a wry grin. "Oh, that would do it," he commented. "I like the way you think, Vickers."

The white-haired man nodded. "You have no idea," he remarked as Jacob tossed the lines off the boat.

Vickers squeezed the grip on the handle to release the locking mechanism on the accelerator. He eased it forward, and the propeller began spinning slowly. The boat moved away from the dock, and Vickers pulled on the rudder stick.

It took several tries and many uncontrolled turns for Vickers to get the feel for the controls. He wouldn't want to race the damned thing through the trees, but he felt more comfortable driving it. By the time he got out of the lake and into the narrower channel, he'd kept the vessel closer to the highlighted route. It would be slow going, but he'd get them there.

TWENTY-SEVEN

We'd made slow time. I'm sure if I'd known the area or traveled it during the daylight, I would have no qualms about speeding through the Glades. But the fastest I felt comfortable with barely crested eight miles per hour. Of course, that was an estimation on my part. This pontoon boat didn't have a speedometer on it.

As the pressure dropped, the air became thicker. Clouds obscured the stars in the sky. A partial moon came up to the south. Despite the relatively clear night, bad weather loomed to the west.

Caleb stood at the bow of the boat, staring out past the lights into the darkness. He was on edge, but it didn't show. If he'd let himself, the man would pace the boat. But he controlled the urge.

I'd seen it before. It's the result of a hurry and wait. War can do that. One minute it's a battle to survive, and then it seems calm. The reality is another fight is around the corner. Adrenaline floods the human body over and over. It becomes an addiction—there's a nervousness, like a meth addict jonesing for his next fix.

This was a bit more than that. He worried about his daughter. Amanda.

I had no frame of reference for that. There were no kids back on *Carina*. She might be the closest thing to a child I have. There's my nephew, but we aren't close. I'd only seen him twice in his fifteen years.

It made me wonder about Caleb. His life before his family marked a stark difference. That existence must have been a lonely one. He moved constantly from task to task, developing no relationships outside of those that served his mission.

Was it much different from my own life? I don't like to stay still. Even when I'm in port, I'm ready to head back out.

I had some relationships, though. Jay. Missy. But, while those were close, they didn't seem to be enough to tie me down to one place.

When I got out of the Corps, I did so for some of the same reasons Caleb did. Not to those extremes. I hadn't seen the corruption of my superiors to any extent. In fact, I wouldn't say I was disillusioned by war or my country's role. Deep down, I'd like to think there existed a difference between the two of us. Unfortunately, I wasn't sure it shined favorably on me.

Caleb switched gears. He gave up that solitary existence for a family. He'd wanted something different—love. After listening to him talk about his son earlier, I realized that he'd found it.

Only to lose it.

No wonder he thought it was the work of karma. Caleb could have been correct. There are people who claim every person has a place—a slot in life. He'd disrupted that natural balance.

Personally, I didn't believe in any of that. Karma didn't exist. I'd seen too many truly bad people living their best lives.

And people can change. Sure, it's a rarity. We as a species fall into habits and lifestyles that are difficult to break. But it can be done.

Caleb did just that.

Now, the result of finding those connections—of learning to love—struck back like a viper. Loss was a bitter pill to swallow. He'd seen his purpose ripped away.

If we didn't save Amanda, I wasn't sure what that might do to the man. He demonstrated a ruthlessness in his killing, and right now he had hope.

Three hours passed, and other than the drone of the motor, the Glades seemed quiet. Every so often, a scream of an airboat somewhere in the distance cried out over the sound of the pontoon's outboard.

We'd disrupted three more alligators as we motored along in the dark. Glowing beads moved away from the light and sound of the motor. They vanished into the dark, not gone. Their presence still lurking out on the edge.

The blue line marking the course we needed to take grew shorter. We still had several miles to go, but the red pin marking our destination signaled the journey ended soon. Most of the time, I felt anticipation when I saw that on *Carina's* chart plotter. It usually meant a hot shower and a meal. Now, it offered a sense of dread.

We followed the train of thought that seemed logical. Xavier took the girl, and there seemed to be only a few places he'd take her. The church or the boathouse. That laid the assumption down that the members of *Las Serpientes* we'd dragged that information out of had been both truthful and knowledgeable enough. I didn't think either Castro or the biker at the church boldly lied to us. It was more likely Xavier, like many leaders of groups like this, kept certain things from his troops. A biker gang might easily turn on its leader if they didn't like his leadership. If I were in such a position, I'd see the value of committing some resources to my own survival. But I'm a pragmatic.

Caleb walked back to the helm and glanced at the screen.

"Can we make a silent approach?" he questioned.

I examined the map. The red pin sat on the edge of a clearing, however there was no way to distinguish how the glades had grown around it. If we made a direct run toward it, any occupants of the house would hear the motor from quite a distance. However, we couldn't run silent. A pontoon boat doesn't row very well. We could do it, but this last mile would take twice as long as the trip so far.

"The only way would be to do so in the water," I advised.

Caleb nodded.

"Yeah, I don't know if you saw how many gators we saw from the boat," I pointed out.

"I did," he admitted.

"Multiply that by twenty," I explained with what I hoped carried a degree of hyperbole.

"Will they attack us?" he asked.

"The ones we've seen so far probably won't," I told him. "That's not a guarantee, though. Even small ones might take a bite. Put them in a group, and it's easy for a frenzy to start."

"You ever seen anything like that?" he asked.

I nodded slowly, remembering a run-in up near Floral City with a man who kept a congregation of alligators penned up so he could toss those who crossed him in for dinner.

"It's a risk I'll take," Caleb said.

He sensed that I wasn't nearly as keen on the idea.

"This is one of their boats," he pointed out. "They might recognize it, so you make the approach. As we get closer, I'll drop off into the water and make my way."

"Either way, something is going to want to kill me," I mused. He stared at me, not sure if I made a joke or not. "Let's do it," I added.

If we weren't going to be quiet, I pressed gently on the throttle, nudging the RPMs up just a fraction. The outboard rumbled a little louder as the bow pushed through the mangroves.

After a few minutes in the overgrowth, the canal debouched into an open lake. Even with only the light of the half moon, I could make out the border of mangroves and trees lining the edge. On the other side of the water, a shape rose off the surface. If the moon hadn't been rising in the sky behind it, the lines of the building would have blended into the vegetation. Instead, six... no, eight posts came out of the water like the legs of an arachnid. Once the supports became visible, my eyes followed them up to the building atop them. The body of this odd little spider appeared circular. Or octagonal. A domed roof with odd edges jutting out from it. It took me a second to realize what I saw—solar panels. The rectangular panels were raised a few inches. In the daylight, the gap between them and the roof would have been more evident.

With my eyes locked on the ominous building, I didn't see Caleb vanish over the side. If I hadn't known what his plan was, I'd have been worried to look over and find my passenger missing in this blackened mire.

The boathouse was dark, and when the powerful LED lights shone across it, I noticed the platform underneath the main floor. Wooden stairs jagged back and forth up to a deck. They'd covered the open deck with the screen. That was the only way it would have been livable in these mosquito-laden waters.

My hand instinctively reached down and touched the G36, leaning against the helm. I wanted to look back and see if Caleb had made it through the water. That would be a bad operational move. Anyone watching from the house would be alerted to his presence.

I was glad it wasn't me traipsing through the muck in waist-deep water with who-knows-what lurking under the water. The real problem was I knew what lurked beneath the black surface. There was little chance I wanted to go in with it.

The house remained still. I throttled back, slowing the motor. The two pontoons coursed through the water slowly as I turned the helm to starboard, letting the boat move parallel to the dock and nestled up against the wood. There were no bumpers on the boat or the dock, and despite the gentleness with which I slid against the structure, the aluminum side clanged as it bounced against the wood.

The dock had two cleats with dock lines that had once been white, but the muddy water had now shaded brown. I secured the line to the bow of the pontoon with a cleat hitch. Before the stern drifted away, I repeated the process on the back with the same knot. On the other corner were two more cleats with brown-stained dock lines.

Where was everyone? It was well after midnight, and if someone waited in the house, they'd surely have heard the approaching motor. At the very least, the bump I made when the boat nudged against the dock was bound to be heard inside. But no one stuck their head out.

I didn't like that at all. If they weren't home, we wasted time coming here, and we weren't close to finding Amanda Harrod. If someone was in the house, they'd know we were coming and be lying in wait.

They could be heavy sleepers, I considered. That didn't seem possible. The swamp was anything but quiet. Most of the noise was natural, but it was loud. Still, the occupants would have grown accustomed to the chirps, howls, and screams of the Everglades' denizens. Something out of that norm would be like ringing an alarm bell. Life on a boat taught me that.

I could sleep in a marina or at anchorage and ignore the obnoxious sounds of halyards clanging, boats motoring, and waves crashing. But throw in a sound I hadn't grown used to, and I'd spring awake. It usually meant something was wrong.

So far, nobody moved in the house. No lights, no doors, nothing. My gut screamed at me, and my brain echoed its sentiment with clanging alarms.

I picked up the G36 and stepped onto the dock. For a second, I peered across the water, looking for Caleb. There were no sounds of thrashing—an excellent sign. Any alligator trying to drag the man to the muddy bottom would make a racket as it fought him. No struggle was a good sign.

With slow, precise steps, I climbed the stairs. The LED lights of the boat only aimed ahead of the pontoon, and they only offered a peripheral glow to show me each step. In the eastern sky, a flash in the distance caught my attention. Was it lightning or had my eyes played a trick on me? I paused on the stairs to search the expanse over the trees on the eastern side of the clearing. A few seconds later, another flash popped. Definitely not a trick of the eyes.

The storm was still miles away. Nothing to get too excited about. Typical Florida weather—it was going to be beautiful weather, break into a storm, then turn pretty again. It happened almost daily somewhere in the state. Some locals joked about how that pattern was required in the state's constitution. A surefire way to send the tourists scattering from the beaches so the people of Florida could enjoy a few minutes of peace.

At the top of the stairs, I rested my hand on the screen door leading into the protected deck. Any minute, the ambush would launch. The G36 lifted to a low ready position as I pulled the door open with my left foot.

Holding the rifle up sent a throbbing pain into my right forearm. Without pausing, I wondered for the countless time whether the bone fractured or the muscle was just sore. Overall, it seemed to heal up quickly, but I didn't think it was enough to warrant doing push-ups yet.

Scattered around the screened porch were hodge-podge furnishings. Old oversized chairs best suited for the side of the curb had been trucked via boat, I assumed. Three ashtrays overflowed with ash and stubbed-out cigarettes. The moisture in the air caked the ash into globs of gray stuff.

As I stepped onto the deck, the screen door behind me slammed.

A high-pitched scream undulated from the house as the door flew open. A figure charged out, firing a twenty-two pistol erratically. Two rounds embedded in the wooden frame securing the screen to the house. Two more landed somewhere else.

I spun the G36 around as I stepped toward the shooter I now recognized as a dark-haired woman. The butt of the rifle cracked against her face, sending her and the pistol scattering back on the deck.

The rifle in my hand came up with the barrel leveled at the darkened door. In the doorway, the woman sprawled unconscious.

TWENTY-EIGHT

The boathouse was empty. At least Amanda Harrod wasn't here. Caleb Saunders
dripped on the plywood floor, leaving puddles
of water seeping through the cracks.

"This is pointless," he bemoaned with more
than an ounce of frustration in his voice. "We
wasted our time."

The man was on edge, and I couldn't gauge
how he would react.

The dark-haired woman stared at me. Her
nose swelled where the gun bashed it in. I wasn't
a doctor, but I guessed I broke it. The thin
cotton dress she wore barely covered her, and
the front carried several blood stains from her
busted face. She'd survive, but right now, she
wasn't happy or cooperative.

"Wasted damned time," he muttered again.

I understood his concern. Time was ticking
past, and we did not know where Amanda was.

Once I established that no one else was in
the shack, Caleb appeared on the stairs, and
we searched the house. The place seemed like
a cross between a trailer park and a hunting
shack. Trash piled up around the rooms, but

it had an organized theme about it. The lack of facilities was similar to my situation aboard my Tartan 40 sailboat. There was no place to throw the trash away. If one were industrious, they would recycle or burn some of it. Here, at least. Fire on a boat is almost always a bad thing, even if it's controlled.

Although, in retrospect, a fire out here would be nearly as debilitating.

"She's not here," Caleb repeated. He was working on the problem in his head. Where did she go? Was she ever here?

I knelt in front of the woman. "Was the girl here?" I asked calmly.

The woman's dark brown eyes flickered, but her lips pursed as if she was refusing to talk. My gut said she'd been here. There wasn't anything to prove it. No baby dolls left behind as the smoking gun. No children's cereal purchased to feed the kid. Not even a grilled cheese left on a plate. If there was a kid here, I didn't see any evidence of it.

But her eyes said something else. The wavering pupils. She locked onto my eyes with a certain stubborn aura I admired. Neither of us intimidated her, and if she got free, her every effort would be to kill us, no matter what. That kind of tenacity was unusual in most people. Normally, when the odds layer up against a person, the instinct for most is to roll over in surrender. Few people are trained to charge up against it. An even smaller number of folks come by that instinct naturally. She seemed like one of those.

The kitchen, though it only barely resembled that, consisted of an old stainless-steel sink. A fifty-five-gallon plastic drum set up as a water-catchment system fed water to the sink on a gravity system. There were two bowls recently washed. The empty can of ravioli sat atop the garbage. Ravioli might be a kid's meal, but it's also easily stored rations. I doubted this woman was out here alone. There was plenty of evidence she had a partner. Men's boxers and shirts hung on a line on the porch. A pair of large flip-flops were beside the unmade bed.

If the woman didn't live here alone, then where was her partner?

"Where is she?" I demanded. If the kid was ever here, it seemed logical she left with the man who lived here. I remembered Castro suggesting Xavier planned to sell the girl. He'd needed a place to stash her. Maybe this was also the meeting point. It's not like it was on any beaten path.

"He took her to get rid of her," Caleb noted. His voice shifted from worried to pragmatic. It must have been tough keeping his mindset on point. He maintained a level head, but the emotion crept up occasionally. I couldn't fault him for that, either.

"I need a few minutes, Chase," Caleb told me.

My gaze lingered on his face. I had a reasonable idea what he had in mind. He didn't believe the woman any more than I did, but he intended to find out the truth.

Nothing about this situation settled well with me. Not that I didn't believe sometimes certain types of torture worked in similar situations. I was on the fence about this one. The woman likely knew something, but I struggled with justifying it. Not my daughter, I reminded myself. If it were, my qualms might not be so prevalent and strong.

I hoped my glare warned him not to overdo it. But I didn't voice it. After all, it wasn't my child. If the only way to save Amanda Harrod was to hurt this woman, I wasn't sure that the decision wouldn't be valid.

My knees straightened, and I walked out onto the porch. Night on the Everglades sang out in a cacophony of insects, increasing breeze, and distant thunder—an elemental orchestra playing, it seemed, for only me. I slouched into one of the grungy overstuffed chairs on the porch. The warm metal of the G36 rested across my knees. Exhaustion crept up on me. I'd planned to be out here in the swamp tonight, but this was supposed to be a relaxing trip with Jay. Instead, the day had taken a different tack altogether.

I let my head roll back against the headrest and let the symphony of nature sound around me. A scream from inside the house indicated Caleb must not have gotten the answer he wanted. Images punctured through my imagination despite my attempts to push them off. It didn't matter that I didn't have a clue what he was doing to her. I envisioned all sorts of possibilities.

As I closed my eyes, I forced any sounds from inside the house out of my mind. In war, sleep came whenever it was available. It didn't matter what was going on. There were times I'd squeeze in ten minutes at a time. Somehow, though, I couldn't let the sleep come over me. Instead, my head lay back with my eyes closed as the sticky air turned cooler. The storm I sensed earlier was pushing inland.

Another squeal of pain filtered out of the door. Despite my best efforts, I couldn't ignore the woman's pain.

The door opened, letting Caleb out onto the deck.

"They took her somewhere," he stated, rubbing something into his hands.

"Did she say where?"

Caleb shook his head. "She told me some guy named Angel took her to meet a guy on a yacht. They left about half an hour before we got here."

"Who's the guy?" I asked.

"She doesn't know. All she said was he sounded like a Middle Easterner. He'll probably take her out of the country, but she isn't sure."

"What kind of boat does he have?" I asked.

"The Middle Easterner?"

"No, her boyfriend. Angel."

He turned and went through the door again. There were no more screams. He stepped out a minute later.

"She doesn't know what kind. A fishing boat."

It was probably similar to the ones we left at the dock in Everglades City. Angel might be familiar enough with the waterways to manage at night, but even if he knew every turn by heart, he wouldn't rush it. Still too many things that can go wrong in the dark, and hopefully, he didn't realize anyone was after him yet.

"Come on," I urged, pushing through the screen door leading down to the pontoon boat.

Caleb followed me, and when I pulled up the map on the chart plotter, I studied the waterway around the Gulf. The water around the eastern tip of Florida is notoriously skinny. Depths stay under four and five feet for close to five miles offshore. Without knowing what kind of yacht Angel was meeting, I had to guess it was one that would comfortably make an Atlantic crossing. That meant it would draw at least four or five feet under its keel.

My finger touched an area just outside of a small bay called First Bay. The depth throughout the tiny inlet was only a foot deep. There was a spot about four and a half miles offshore where a boat could drop anchor in eight or nine feet of water. With the storm coming off the Gulf, it would be a rough ride overnight, but the holding in that area was a good sand and mud mixture which would secure the anchor tightly.

"This is the closest anchorage to here," I explained. "With that storm coming in, it's unlikely they'll pull anchor until morning when the weather has passed."

"Are you sure?" he questioned.

I shrugged. "I can't be sure. There's nothing to go on but common sense. I have sailed up this side of the state and anchoring out there is tough. The captain of the yacht will ideally wait for the right window to pull anchor. In fact, I'd bet Angel waits out the weather there too. He will not want to fight his way back in this storm."

"Let's go," he demanded.

I nodded as I started the outboard. Caleb untied the bow line as I pulled the stern line aboard. The light bar on the awning came on, illuminating the surface of the water. Easing the throttle down, I motored off the dock. It took a minute to set the course. The chart plotter mapped the best route through the mangroves to First Bay. They did not mark this in the history like the journey from Everglades City to here. We'd risk hitting areas impassable in this boat.

Even with that concern in the back of my mind, I gave the outboard more gas, increasing our speed. I knew what I told Caleb, but doubts flooded my brain. If the storm stalled, the captain might try to pull anchor and beat it south to get out of the path of the weather. Or I could be wrong entirely about where the rendezvous would be. It made sense. Logically, Angel would want to make the trip as expediently as possible. But that was still only a guess on my part.

We pushed through the first channel leading off the lake where the boathouse stood. A screaming engine announced itself in the distance. Caleb heard it at the same time as me. He turned to look my direction.

"Is that him coming back already?" he asked with worry in his eyes.

I shook my head, pulling the throttle back so the outboard only idled. "That's coming from behind us," I told him. "And that's an airboat."

"Are they usually out this late?" he asked.

"Some are," I admitted. "But that one's coming closer."

"They're after me," he suggested.

Without a second thought, I throttled the engine up. The outboard whined but even its sound didn't drown out the shriek of the airboat behind us. We maneuvered through the channel, shifting from one side to the other as trees and logs came into view.

The boat jerked to a stop for a split second as the port pontoon rode up over a submerged log. Inertia, along with an extra boost on the throttle, pushed us over the fallen tree. When the boat was free, the propeller shot us forward as the noise of the other boat silenced. I realized too late they stopped to pinpoint our direction. As I reached to pull the engine back to idle, the scream resounded across the swamp.

Bright lights illuminated the channel two hundred yards behind us. With the outboard motor giving us all the juice it could, we raced forward. I wondered for a second if Jay was on that boat with the Federal agents chasing us. It was only a passing thought which vanished when the first round pinged off the aluminum frame.

I dropped behind the helm as more gunfire erupted behind us.

TWENTY-NINE

A pontoon boat has the maneuverability of a boulder. I jerked the wheel starboard, but even with the motor running wide open, the boat only turned slowly at a small angle. Caleb raised his M4, returning fire. I reached up and cut the lights on the awning. Caleb and I plunged into darkness. Behind us, the airboat cast an LED beam on us. Shadows stretched around us.

"Shoot out the light," I suggested as I spun the wheel back and forth. The pontoon made a wide S-shaped journey from one side of the canal to the other. The only light on the boat now was the glow of the chart plotter, which was all I had to steer us by. I turned the screen so it was visible from the under the helm. There was no point trying to stare out into the darkness. I would only give whoever was shooting at us a target.

Based on the chart plotter, the channel was narrowing before it opened into a bigger river.

"We can't outrun them," I shouted at Caleb, who paused his return fire long enough to re-load a magazine.

Gunfire peppered the stern of the boat. They seemed to outgun us as well.

"Ideas?" he asked.

"Be ready to unload on them," I told him. "Then get off the damn boat."

We were far enough out of their beam of light that they'd have a hard time seeing us until they closed in on us. For now, they were just shooting wildly into the dark. But at their speed, it would take seconds to catch us.

It seemed like a good idea to let them. As the waterway narrowed, I cut the throttle and turned to port. The pontoon lost momentum, but the turned motor acted like a rudder, spinning the boat sideways in the channel.

"Shoot the light," I repeated to Caleb as I raised the G36 and let out a barrage at the shining eye in the black.

Both of our guns flashed in the dark as we unloaded a magazine into the light. It blinked out, and in the darkness, the scream of the boat raced toward us.

"Jump!" I shouted as I threw myself over the stern and outboard.

When the crash sounded, it seemed to shake the water and the trees with a screech of metal on metal. I surfaced as the airboat careened over the pontoon, rotating in the air and slamming down on its side. I straightened my legs to find myself in four feet of water. The G36 came up in my arms, barrel directed at the airboat, which skidded to a stop on a small embankment. A flash of lightning illuminated the hulking vessel. The prop still howled as it spun without moving the boat.

There was no sign of Caleb. I didn't like the idea of being in the water in the dark, but I hoped the crash sent anything bigger than me swimming away. My feet trudged along the mucky bottom toward the airboat. Another bolt of lightning creased across the sky as the wind picked up. In the split second of light, I surveyed the pontoon. The hull of the other boat crushed the starboard side when it rode up over it. It wasn't listing at all, which was surprising, but the aluminum pontoons should hold the rest afloat if they didn't fill with water. As long as any damage to the tubes was above the waterline, it would float. I'd need to check the motor and controls to see if they worked properly.

Right now, the increasing wind pushed the derelict boat away from me. I needed to find Caleb and confirm our attackers were neutralized before I worried about the boat.

The next bolt of lightning revealed a figure moving along the embankment. I thought there was a white head, but it might have been a trick of light. As I eased my way to the shore, I tried to make no noise. The shooter in the other boat could be injured or even unarmed at the moment, but I had to assume he was waiting for one of us to give away our location.

Did Caleb make it off the boat before the impact? I still didn't see him.

"Aaa!" a primal scream erupted as a flash of silver sliced through the air to my left.

I twisted, raising the G36 to block the blade. In the dark, a thin figure swiped at me again. He reminded me of a robot at first, until I realized he was wearing night vision goggles. I jumped back as he thrust the blade forward. The knife sliced my hand before it struck the metal of the G36 again, this time knocking it out of my grip. The gun fell beneath the surface, and I dove back before he stabbed me.

My body sank in the three feet of water, and I pushed my feet off my attacker, propelling me away from him. Underwater was pitch black. Even when I opened my eyes, there was nothing but darkness. I couldn't stay down forever, and there wasn't a way to circle around him. In shallow water like this, they could see any movement I made above the surface. Instead, I sank to the bottom, motionless.

I could hold my breath for a long time. Years of training in the Corps built up a stamina. Couple that with years of snorkeling and free-diving gave me several minutes before I'd need to surface. I'd just play like an alligator and wait. Eventually, he'd want to get away for fear I was planning something. Or he might assume he got a good strike in, leaving me dead somewhere.

Instead, the idiot assumed the night vision gave him the upper hand. I felt the muddy bottom shift as he shuffled near me. His feet squished into the bottom, sending trapped air out a hundred different directions. The water moved around me, and I knew he was close.

I sprang up, catching him in the crotch and erupting out of the water. The two of us crashed back under the surface, only I was now on his back. My weight drove him down to the bottom.

The man thrashed, trying to slice me with his knife. He could not twist away from me to get the momentum or target he needed. My left hand was still stronger right now, and I caught the back of his head and pressed it down into the mud. My legs pressed down on his back, applying all my weight. Without being able to get enough traction to push up, he flailed under my weight for several seconds as I buried his face deeper into the silt. My lungs were burning by the time he stopped moving. I raised my head above the water and gulped some air before going back under again.

My arms wrapped around what I was sure was his lifeless neck. With a quick wrench, I snapped the vertebrae in his neck, ensuring he was truly lifeless. My right arm hurt again. Worse than before. I lifted the arm as a bolt of lightning creased from the low-hanging clouds inching over. A tree on the opposite side of the channel exploded like a firecracker. The blast of light illuminated a carved bone handle sticking out of my forearm. The bastard stuck me in the struggle.

Black liquid drizzled down my arm and dripped into the equally black water. The wind whistled down the channel, followed by the sound of a freight train. I glanced away from the knife to a wall of rain pushing up the river.

The torrential downpour pelted me, washing away the blood as fast as it poured out of the wound.

I hadn't passed out yet, which I counted as positive. If the blade sliced either the radial or the brachial arteries, I'd have lost consciousness by now. Unless the blade was pinching the vessels closed. Too often, a victim pulls the blade out without thinking, and the result is a sudden blood loss previously staunched off by the injuring implement.

Get to shore, Gordon. I slogged my feet forward toward the overturned airboat. With lightning striking so close, I wanted out of the water. While I knew little about alligators, I didn't want to entice one with my blood. They might not be like sharks, but in certain cases, it is always better to err on the side of caution.

Where was Caleb? If he'd surfaced after the crash, I hadn't seen him.

I dropped onto my ass in the mud and ripped the bottom of my shirt with my left hand. The wet fabric came away in a large swath. I'd hoped to get a thin strip, but with only one hand working the fabric, it was wider than I intended. It shouldn't matter. My left hand wound the muddy strip around my arm just above the knife. After pulling it tight, I swallowed hard as I reached to pull the blade from my arm.

As painful as a blade driving into one's arm might be, removing it always seems to hurt more. Usually, by then, the adrenaline has receded, and like in my case, I was fully aware of it. While I had barely noticed the stabbing amid the underwater struggle.

When I pulled the handle out, I pulled on the tourniquet with my teeth, trying to tighten more. There's a pulling sensation coupled with removing something like that. The blade seems to cut through more muscle as it comes back out. Sometimes when the knives have serrated blades or barbs, the damage coming out is worse than the going in. Luckily, this was a straight dagger, so while it hurt, the blade slid out easily.

"Where is Corsair?" a voice shouted behind me.

I twisted around to see a figure with white hair looming over me. A Glock 19 aimed at me, looking ominous in the flashes of lightning. Rain dripped off the barrel in a steady stream as it poured over the man. Black streaks mixed in the white hair, making the man look like a zebra.

My left hand tightened around the bone handle. I couldn't use it with any effectiveness. By the time I got it up to throw it, he'd pull the trigger.

So, I shook my head. "He went into the river," I told him.

The zebra scowled. His eyes flicked toward the river. He cocked his head to the side as he decided I had nothing to offer him. I stared up at the barrel when the first round grazed him.

Zebra spun around, firing upriver at a mass of white light flying across the water like a spirit. The Angler 204 emerged from the sheets of rain. I rolled away from Zebra and scampered to my feet as he fired at the boat. I ran behind the airboat, finding cover from the gunfire. When I looked back, I couldn't make out who was driving the boat. I assumed it was Jay, but a figure on the bow continued shooting at the shoreline. I saw Zebra drop on one knee and fire on the figure. Even in the storm and mayhem, I watched the form drop off the front. The boat skidded to a stop and spun around.

In the glow of the dash lights, I made out Jay's features. My feet moved as I charged around the boat toward Zebra. I threw the knife in my hand at the mass of white hair glowing in the dark. He flinched, and I thought I might have hit him. He didn't drop, but turned to fire at me.

Gunfire erupted behind him as Caleb appeared with the M4 in his hand. The muzzle flashed in a staccato of flares. Zebra's body convulsed as each round ripped through him. I watched him collapse forward. His body splashed in the puddles of mud and water.

THIRTY

Jay Delp hit the spotlight on the helm, searching for Hubbard in the black water. Hubbard spotted Vickers's white hair in the distance. Jay gunned the engine when she reported he was holding Chase at gunpoint. She started firing at the man, trying to draw him away from Chase.

When he returned fire, it was with a precision even Jay wasn't sure he could repeat. Hubbard vanished from the bow, and Jay reacted as quickly as he could. The boat's momentum carried the hull across the water even after he cut the power. He realized he was putting himself in Vickers's sights, but he needed to find Hubbard.

In the back of his mind, he heard the gunfire, but he scanned the water for Hubbard. There was no sign of the agent, but the lights glistened off two beady eyes moving across the water toward the area where Hubbard went under.

Jay's forty-five came up, and he fired at the gator moving across the water. Three shots sent the alligator in the other direction.

Something floated in the water about fifty yards away. Jay turned the wheel on the helm and pointed the front toward the flotsam. He eased the throttle forward and puttered toward it. It was the back of Hubbard's shirt. He pulled the motor into neutral and slid into the water. His arms wrapped around the agent's body, and he lifted her out of the water. With his left hand on the gunwale, he pulled up and heaved Hubbard onto the boat.

Her chest was red from the round. Vickers hit her in the left torso. The bullet missed her heart, but he was sure it shredded her left lung. He needed to stabilize her. His hands ripped the shirt open. The wound was just over her left breast. He snipped the bra with his knife.

Under the helm, his first aid kit hung inside the control panel. He ripped it open and pulled the bottle of isopropyl alcohol out. The liquid doused the wound thoroughly. Jay worried her fall in the river would introduce contamination. The clear liquid washed away the blood, only for more to seep out. Once he thought he'd cleaned it as well as he could, he applied several layers of gauze, holding pressure on the wound.

The Angler 204 twisted in the wind as he worked. He tried to ignore the spiraling motion as the cotton soaked with blood. He pressed tighter, adding a couple more layers of pads on top before ripping several strips of medical tape from a roll to secure the bandage.

While he held his palm against the bandage to maintain pressure, his right hand reached up for the VHF radio.

"Mayday, Mayday, Mayday!" he shouted into the microphone.

After several seconds of silence, he repeated, "Mayday, Mayday, Mayday. Officer needs assistance."

There was no answer, then a voice crackled over the speaker. "Jay, what's your sitrep?" Chase asked over the radio.

"Agent Hubbard has been shot in the chest. I've got pressure on the bleeding, but she needs a hospital."

"Go!" Chase urged. "We've secured this."

"What about the girl?" Jay asked.

"She's being taken on a yacht. Get her to a hospital. Call in the Coast Guard, too."

"What yacht?" he asked.

"We don't know," Chase admitted. "We'll get there."

"Roger," Jay acknowledged.

"You won't be able to go through the Gulf. Too rough. Backtrack," Chase told him.

With two fingers, he checked Hubbard's pulse. It was steady, but her breathing remained labored. He moved her gently, so she lay beside him. Once she was closer, he propped her head with a life preserver and used two other life jackets on either side of her to prevent her from rolling to the side.

After he was confident she wouldn't move, he grabbed the radio. "Are you sure you don't need a lift?"

"Caleb's going after his daughter no matter what," Chase explained. "I'll back him up as best as I can."

"Flash, if I don't get word from you, I'm coming back."

"Go!"

Jay pressed the throttle down and turned the wheel slowly, rotating the bow around before he gunned the machine. Within seconds, the Angler vanished in the storm.

THIRTY-ONE

"We need that boat," Caleb insisted.

"He's got to get that agent to help," I told him.

"The agent trying to kill me?" he asked.

"Jay wouldn't do anything he didn't think he needed to do."

"That's bullshit!" Caleb exclaimed. "We don't have time."

I studied the man, his desperation shining through.

"We need to right this airboat," I urged.

He stared up at the aluminum hull resting on its port gunwale. The prop had stopped spinning when I shut the motor off while talking to Jay on the VHF. His eyes turned to my arm, bound with muddy cloth. His head shook. "We need to get that arm tended to first," he pointed out, his voice mellowing.

He opened several compartments on the overturned boat until a small white box fell out. We huddled under the protection of the airboat while he stripped the muddy bandage off my arm. He used the alcohol to clean the wound and bound the wound tightly with a white gauze bandage. He ripped a strap off one of the orange Mae West life vests and created a sling to hold the arm against my torso.

Once my arm was immobile, Caleb pulled a Danworth anchor with the hinged flukes. He hooked the flukes on the starboard gunwale that was upright. The fifty-foot rope attached to the anchor shackle flew over the boat, and I caught it with my good arm. The line stretched out until I looped it around the base of a gumbo limbo tree. Caleb helped me attach it to my waist so I could pull it with just my left hand and the weight of my body. When he was ready, I began heaving the line with my body. Caleb used a small log to pry under the port side, lifting it off the mud. After several tries, the boat tumbled over, righting itself.

It took both of us pushing the bow of the boat to ease the hull back into the water. Once the boat was afloat, we climbed aboard.

"You'll need to drive," I told him. "It needs both hands."

Caleb nodded, climbing into the raised captain's seat. The engine roared to life, and he eased the boat away from the shoreline. The rain continued to pelt me, and as the boat sped up, the drops stung like needles piercing me. I shielded my eyes with my left hand before I lost my footing, realizing I needed my one usable arm to hang on.

When someone who is used to operating a boat finds himself not only in the passenger's seat but also somewhat helpless, he doesn't enjoy being out of control. What I mean is that I felt like I was out of control.

Caleb was a master behind the controls, deftly guiding the airboat along. I held onto the helm, watching the chart plotter as he followed the course on the screen. The wind coming up the river created a heavy chop, and the hull pitched back and forth as Caleb pressed it forward.

After a few minutes of needling rain punching at my face, I turned to face behind me. The pelting continued on my back, but at least the sting wasn't blinding me. Instead of watching ahead, I resorted to studying the wake behind us as it spread out in the dark of night and rain.

The channel opened up, and I risked a glance, shielding my face with my left arm. The bay could hardly be called a bay. At best, it was an inlet impeded mostly by washed out logs and fallen boughs piling up after every rain pushed the debris out to sea. A small island extended from the northern shore of the bay almost two-thirds of the way across. The southern pass was only a foot deep, according to the charts. With the tide heading out and the wind blowing in, the waves almost appeared to be churning like a washing machine.

"Can we fit through there?" Caleb asked, pointing at the water.

Typically, the answer would have been yes. The airboat only drew a few inches, and the chart's recorded depths were normally taken at low tide. Still, the weather can do crazy things to the sea. A low-pressure system can suck the water away from the shore like it has a straw, or it can surge it back as it blows it back. I nodded either way. The worst case was we run aground. Well, that wasn't the worst case, but there was no point in dwelling on anything too drastic.

"Not too fast," I urged, as he pointed the bow toward the pass.

The bow sloshed under a wave, spraying salt-water over us. Briny droplets covered my lips. On the other side of the pass, the depth remained a little less than two feet. We skipped across the surface without worry.

"There," Caleb called, extending a finger across the water.

In this weather, I struggled to determine how far away the light we saw sat. Three to four miles. It was indistinguishable in the sheets of rain, but the two bright lights broke through the rain. There were no other lights on the horizon.

It still seemed like such a long shot. I understood how it made sense the yacht we were looking for would be here. Somehow, it surprised me when we found something. Despite my hope, realism stuck to my gut. Until we got closer, there was no way to be sure.

But Caleb seemed positive. His countenance lifted as soon as he spotted the lights. Of course, there were always lights. Fishermen, cruisers, buoys, and channel markers. Not to mention the countless lights from houses sitting on the end of a peninsula, scorning sailors like tricksters of old.

As we moved out of the somewhat protected waters of the little bay, the wind and waves whipped the surface into a frenzy. An airboat

was suddenly a terrible vessel for the open sea.
I suspected as much before we took it. The
narrow beam combined with the length and
lightweight material in the hull meant a rogue
wave might flick it like the lucky ace during the
last draw.

Airboats have a specific design—to move easily over skinny, swampy waters filled with debris. The propeller on the back of the boat
pushes the air and applying some fundamen-
tal of physics I never bothered to learn. The
result is the hull can skim over the surface at
high speeds, all while avoiding the pesky things,
like the bottom, under the water. What airboats
aren't designed for is traversing open water
with six-foot seas blowing back.

It might have been one of the longest hours of
my life. In part, I was helpless. It was the same
thing we all dealt with eventually—watching
someone less experienced doing something we
all feel we would be more adept at doing. Unfortunately, the airboat required both hands,
and I was useless.

Every time the bow dove into a trough, the
prop only pushed the front into the next wave.
When we climbed over the wave, the water in
the boat sloshed aft. The sudden shift in weight
sank the stern into the water, and the motor
proved almost completely ineffectual.

"We're going to swamp!" I warned Caleb.

The man remained focused on the lights on
the yacht, but his brow furrowed. If the rain
and sea hadn't drenched us to the bone, I was
certain I would have seen beads of sweat on his

brow. Although despite the strain and stress, he appeared stoic and intent.

The rudders on the propeller swiveled starboard, then port, then starboard again as he struggled to keep the vessel moving through the chop. After twenty minutes, the outline of the yacht became more clear. It was a flybridge model with a large domed radar on the top. While the boat was at least fifty feet, it was hard to distinguish in the weather. Flashes of lightning behind left the split-second image burned in my memory. Its bow stretched out with a large forward deck. On the stern, a swim platform jutted out at the water's surface. Large bulbous fenders hung lazily off the railings. Sloppy captain. Proper boatmanship required the bumpers to be stowed while the vessel was away from the dock. Maybe they'd left the dock earlier and intended to head back to the pier in the morning. It was still lazy, but at least the efficiency factor could be justified.

Above the swim platform, a small inflatable dinghy hung from two davits. The next flash of lightning revealed another boat tied to the port side—a shallow draft fishing boat. It was exactly the kind of boat we'd seen at the dock in Everglades City. The type perfect for cruising the backwaters of the Glades. While not as badly designed for the open water as the airboat, its low profile made it easily swamped.

"That's it," I confirmed, nodding toward the fishing boat. "No way that boat came with the yacht."

I was pretty sure I saw a slight grin pass over Caleb's face. With a hundred yards to go, he pulled the throttle back.

"What are you doing?" I questioned as the sudden loss of momentum left the airboat vulnerable to the crashing waves.

"He'll hear us," he pointed out.

I couldn't argue with him. The airboat's engine screamed like a banshee. It was possible they'd already heard us churning across the sea. However, the storm likely covered the sound. If we got much closer, though, it would be obvious.

Caleb strapped the M4 to his back before checking a nine-millimeter he'd picked up somewhere. He stripped off his shirt, winding the Glock in it and tying it up like a bag. Then he attached the makeshift satchel to his pants.

"I'll make the approach," he informed me. "Give me thirty minutes and ease over to the yacht. By then, it won't matter if they hear you coming."

"I can make the swim," I assured him.

He pointed at my injured arm. "I can't worry about you keeping up," he told me. "Whoever's on the boat, I can handle."

Begrudgingly, I nodded. The side line has always been the last place I wanted to be. But Caleb made sense. While I didn't doubt I could hold my own, even in my injured state, I might be a distraction to Caleb, who didn't really know my capabilities.

Caleb climbed to the front of the boat and dove into the water. With all the lights on the airboat extinguished, I quickly lost sight of him as he swam out of view. I wrapped my functional arm around the captain's chair as the boat rocked back and forth.

The wind was blowing from the west at about fifty knots, and I expected the airboat to be washed up toward shore in less than an hour. There was no way I could just float out here while I waited. After five minutes, I figured I'd given Caleb enough time to get away from the boat. If I'd been in any other boat, it might be easy to keep the outboard idling or barely in gear to maintain some steering capabilities.

Airboats don't work as easily. I started the motor, applied enough throttle to push the boat slowly, and then used my left hand to control the rudders, pulling and pushing on the controls to swivel the rudders. I attempted to make wide S-shaped paths through the waves. As I made my sixth turn back south, a rogue wave rose under the bow. I pulled back on the rudder control, but the wave twisted the hull around. The boat flopped down on the starboard side as a second wave crashed over the gunwale and pushed the starboard side under. Before I could give the engine more throttle, hoping to push the boat out of the trough, the boat fell in. A third wave swamped the vessel.

In what felt like a slow-motion twirl, the airboat rotated over. As lightning lit up the area, I saw the water just milliseconds before I went under, the aluminum hull crashing down on top of me.

THIRTY-TWO

Corsair swam through the black, salty waters just under the surface. Each breath he stole was quick and deep, filling his lungs like a gas tank. His controlled breathing had atrophied little in the last ten years. Each gulp of air was enough to cover a hundred feet. There wasn't as much concern about the occupants of the boat seeing him. The storm provided the perfect cover. He could come up for air between waves and vanish again before anyone could see him.

Once he was closer to the yacht, he studied the target. The white hull loomed in the dark. *L'étoile*, the lettering on the stern read.

The star, Caleb, translated in his head.

Deck lights lit up the boat, and the owner installed purple LED lighting just under the waterline. It illuminated the yacht clearly, but if anyone looked out, they'd be able to see Caleb swimming close. He'd have to risk it. Most likely, everyone chose to be tucked in tightly, weathering the storm with a cocktail.

Was Amanda onboard? For the first moment since this day began, he felt a glimmer of hope.

Corsair pushed that ray down. No time to dwell on dreams of "What if?" Stay on task, he reminded himself.

It was more than just trying to focus on the mission. Corsair had seen missions fail. Usually at worst, someone who should have died escapes with their life. This wasn't a mission Corsair had the luxury of failing. If Amanda was on the yacht, Caleb either left with her or he didn't leave at all.

Lightning flashed across the sky as Corsair sank below the surface. He dropped ten feet. Fifteen. In the hazy dark water, the purple glow called to him. His feet pedaled as he swam toward the light. He hung below the boat for several seconds. A slight singe developed in his lungs. He took his time. Carefully, he removed the shirt he'd fashioned into a bag and unwound it in the dark.

Don't drop it, he thought to himself.

While the water was only twelve feet deep, he would never find the Glock in the dark if it slipped from his grip. His hand wrapped around the grip. The back strap nestled into his palm, and his index finger tightened around the trigger guard. The shirt drifted away. In the glow of the purple light, it reminded Caleb of a jellyfish lurking alone. He touched the M4 with his left hand, reassuring himself the rifle was still there.

He kicked toward the swim platform hanging off the stern. Caleb's head rose slowly. The barrel of the Glock came out of the water simultaneously. He blinked twice, clearing the droplets of saltwater from his eyelashes.

No one was on the back of the boat. He didn't expect there to be, but Corsair believed in assuming the worst was coming.

He pushed up on his forearms and rolled onto the swim platform. On his belly, he crawled under the dinghy until he emerged on the other side. Crouched against the transom, Corsair lifted his head over the edge. The aft deck was empty. Water pooled as rain gushed back from other parts of the vessel. A towel left on deck had washed into the port scupper, clogging the drain. The starboard side was clear, but with the yawl of the vessel, most of the water wanted to go to the port side. It wasn't a concern. Only if it stormed for a week or two, but he doubted that would even do anything.

The aft deck covered about a hundred square feet. Centered on the deck, a stainless-steel table with seating for six offered plenty of space for outdoor dining. A four-man hot tub bubbled on the port side.

A sliding glass door led from the deck into the galley. Corsair lowered himself below the railing, so a flash of lightning didn't give away his silhouette. All the interior lights were lighted up. He observed as a Middle Eastern man crossed from the salon to the galley. The man opened a full-sized stainless-steel refrigerator and pulled a bottle of white wine from a rack. The bottle had already been corked, and the man opened it. Corsair imagined the popping sound the bottle made when the cork came free. The label faced away, but from the color, he presumed it was a Chardonnay. The gold liquid poured just a little thicker than a lighter Sauvignon Blanc or Pinot Grigio. It could have been some other grape popularized in the last decade while Corsair was gone. It was easy to assume the bottle was expensive. A man with a ship like this vessel didn't skimp on wine, even if he didn't know the difference between White Zinfandel and a pink Moscato.

Caleb restrained himself from charging through the glass door. He wanted to know Amanda was here. Despite the pain he endured today, the logical part of his brain reminded him that this could be an innocent party just waiting out the storm.

Corsair would play it out. *L'étoile* wasn't pulling anchor at the moment. As long as no one stepped out on the back deck for a smoke, he could wait here and observe.

The man with the wine walked back toward the salon. Corsair straightened to peer around the room. An L-shaped sofa stared out the glass doors. Had the man with the wine been sitting there, he'd be staring right at Corsair. Another sofa sat against the starboard edge of the salon.

Behind the L-shaped sofa two steps went up to the galley, which took up half the cabin with a counter extending into the salon area. A small stove and oven sat next to the refrigerator. Beyond it, another counter jutted out with a stainless steel sink. Large glass windows surrounded the salon offering at least a 180-degree view, albeit the view was not consecutive.

White leather settees and seats covered the other half of the cabin. At the long settee on the starboard wall, a glass dining table sat. The man with the Chardonnay set his glass down on the table as he settled onto the leather cushions. The Middle Easterner turned as a curly haired gorilla lumbered up the steps leading down to the berths. He was clearly Latino, with a bushy beard and hair extending past his shoulders. He was wearing a white tank top. A water stain crept up from the bottom of the shirt as if the man hung it up but put it back on before it finished drying.

The man could have passed for one of the bikers. He hadn't seen Amanda yet, but the biker's presence bolstered his confidence. He checked the Glock when he saw the biker answer a cell phone. The bearded face twisted as he talked. Could the woman have gotten free at the boathouse? She might call him to warn him someone was coming. Or it could be another biker spreading the word about what happened at the church?

No point in wasting any more time. He raised the barrel of the nine-millimeter and straightened up when a flash of lightning washed across the sky like a full second of daylight. The bearded biker's eyes widened when he saw a man on board the boat.

"*¡Cuidado!*" the biker shouted, dropping the phone as he pulled a thirty-eight revolver from behind him.

Corsair's feet shifted with the pitch of the deck. As the sliding glass door exploded, he seemed to glide across the deck, landing behind the stainless-steel table on his shoulders. He squeezed the trigger twice, firing at the man as he stepped toward the opening. Both rounds hit the refrigerator past the man, but it stopped the biker from coming farther onto the deck.

Watch the shots, Caleb reminded himself. Amanda was somewhere on board.

He kicked his foot up, catching the underside of the table and flipping it forward. With a shield wall made of sixteen-gauge stainless-steel, he could hold out for a while. A thirty-eight-caliber bullet wouldn't punch through even if it were armor piercing. It was a safe bet the biker wasn't carrying a special load like that.

He forgot those two rounds Corsair used to warn him away. The biker extended his hand out the door, firing at the table. Bullets pinged, seemingly before the gun fired. It was all in his head. He knew that. He might have been hearing the previous round or an echo. Time slowed itself in a fight like this.

"Who is it?" the Middle Eastern man asked.

"Fuck if I know," the biker howled.

Caleb leaned back against the table. He just wanted to get Amanda and leave.

"I want the girl," he stated loudly so his voice would carry through the storm.

"You the bastard that burned down the club," the biker demanded.

"Yeah," Corsair responded. "Killed a whole mess of you snakes."

The biker screamed and pulled the trigger. The table reverberated as six rounds struck the top.

Six rounds. He was empty. Corsair twisted around the side of the table and fired three quick shots. The biker fell back, but Corsair was certain he'd only pegged him in the leg.

The biker howled something in Spanish as a roll of thunder barreled through the clouds overhead. Caleb heard the tinkle of shells hitting the deck. He was reloading.

"Let him have her," the Middle Eastern man demanded.

"No!" the biker shouted. "He killed my friends."

"They killed my family," Caleb shouted back pointedly.

"Fuck you!" the biker shouted, and he fired three shots out the door.

He didn't hit the table. Corsair considered the layout he'd seen. He knew the man had a bullet in his leg. At least one. He wasn't standing. Panicked, he would retreat behind the L-shaped sofa.

"Just give me my daughter," Caleb insisted. "I'll leave you alone."

"The hell I will," the Guatemalan retorted. "What if I kill her first?"

Corsair responded, "I'll kill you and that Arab fucker. I'll sink this damned boat and swim back to that little house in the swamp where I'll spend at least twelve hours carving parts off your girlfriend. After that, I'll hunt down every family member you have until I know there isn't the slightest chance any part of you survives."

No one said anything. Other than the raging storm, which for the most part became little more than white noise to Corsair, there was no sound.

He'd made threats like that before. He always meant them—to a degree. Today, he knew he was telling the truth. He was angry. In a way, he'd never felt before. Every fiber of his body was pulsing with rage. If somehow he'd gotten this close to his daughter to watch some asshole murder her in front of him, he'd let loose on the world a hurt unlike a vengeance anyone had seen before.

"You can have her," the Arabic man announced.

"No!"

"She's mine now," the man argued to the biker. "I can do with her as I wish."

"He'll kill us," the biker insisted.

"No, I won't," Caleb promised.

"I don't bel—"

The sentence was punctuated with gunfire. Corsair held his breath for a second, steadying his heartbeat for what might come next.

"You can have her," the Arabic man stated.

There was no dissent from the Guatemalan. Corsair tightened his grip on the Glock as he lifted it over the table. The Middle Eastern man held his hands above his head. On the floor beside him was a Beretta Px4. As he stepped around the table, the dead biker's head lolled to the side with a dribble of blood dripping like drool from the corner of his mouth.

"She's down below," he informed Corsair.

"Is she hurt?"

The man shook his head. "She was in fine shape," he told him with the same mannerisms as a man selling a car.

A man selling a car. That was exactly what the man sounded like. He'd said it a few seconds earlier. "She'd mine now. I can do with her as I wish." He'd treated his daughter like an object. Caleb swallowed hard when a wave of thoughts washed through his head. What would she have endured because of this man? Would he have sold her to someone else? He'd seen men in Afghanistan with harems of women. They were as interchangeable as shoes for people like that. Even *Las Serpientes* considered her only chattel to be traded. Corsair knew that depravity stretched not just through the Mid-East and the swamps of Florida, but through the world.

Still, he didn't want to imagine his daughter in this man's hands. He didn't want to imagine anyone's daughter in his hands.

"Sorry, I lied," Corsair told the man as he raised the Glock to his head and squeezed the trigger. The man fell back, striking the glass table. The tempered glass exploded into shards and pebbles.

Premature, Corsair scolded himself. What if he'd lied and Amanda wasn't on board?

He climbed down the stairs, still holding the Glock. He was becoming acutely aware that he didn't have a shirt on. The chill of the air conditioning drew goose bumps on his skin as he opened the door to the first cabin. On the twin bed, Amanda Harrod pressed herself against the corner with her knees pressed against her chest. Her cheeks were stained with the salt from dried tears. She stared up at the door, and when her eyes recognized her daddy, they brightened.

"Daddy!" she bounded off the bed and ran to him. Caleb dropped the Glock and stepped into the cabin and wrapped his arms around her.

Caleb kissed his daughter, and she squeezed his neck.

"Where's Mama?" his daughter asked, with her face buried in his neck.

He didn't want to tell her right then. Truth be told, he never wanted to tell her. Instead, he held her in his arms, silent tears streamed down his face.

For the first time since he'd heard the first gunshot this morning, time seemed to catch up to itself. Maybe it even picked up speed. After some time, he loosened his grip on Amanda, kissing her salty cheeks. He picked her up in his arms and straightened. The girl wrapped her arms around his neck.

"Can we go home, Daddy?" she asked.

Caleb thought about Chase. "We need to meet a friend of mine first," he told her as he carried her out of the cabin. "I want you to close your eyes for me, though. Keep them closed until I tell you it's okay to open them."

"'Kay Daddy," she agreed, squeezing her eyes tightly closed. Wrinkles creased out from the corners of her eyelids. Caleb smiled, almost laughing.

He climbed the three steps into the salon and froze. A thin Guatemalan man with jet black hair stared back at him. He held a Smith & Wesson forty-five leveled at Caleb. A colorful viper crawled down his arms so that it appeared the gun was nestled in the viper's mouth.

"The dad?" the man who seemed to be in his fifties.

Caleb nodded, trying to calculate how to protect Amanda. The Glock was still in Amanda's cabin, and the M4, while strapped to his back, was inaccessible. If the man shot, his bullet would tear through Amanda before striking Caleb's heart.

"You are a big fucking pain in the ass," the man told him. "I don't guess I totally blame you, but I can't let you leave here."

"Sure you can," Caleb argued. "Maybe we are at a point where we let bygones be bygones."

"Do I look like the forgiving type?" he asked.

"Let my girl go, please," Caleb begged.

The man blinked. Caleb couldn't tell if he was considering it. When the man's pupils dilated, Caleb twisted around, throwing Amanda down the stairs as the Smith & Wesson fired. Caleb fell down the steps. The last thing he saw was his daughter's screaming face. The last thing he did was brace his arms in front of him so he didn't crush the girl.

THIRTY-THREE

I tried to dive, but the overturned hull did a quicker job of shoving me under. The sound of a balloon popping echoed under the surface. Despite being stunned, I kicked down away from the debris dumping to the sea floor from the airboat.

When I surfaced, I twisted to see the boat drifting away from me. Flotsam, ranging from life vests to fishing bobbers, floated around me. Survival experts advise staying with the swamped boat—it was equipped with positive flotation which would keep it afloat for a while. However, where it floated was another question altogether.

No, my best bet was to make it to the yacht. Normally, that swim would take me ten minutes, even in this weather. However, with one arm still bound to my chest, it would be a little slower. I could at least keep it in a straight line.

The quickest way to get there seemed to be underwater. Since I was relying on my feet mostly, it wouldn't matter much. This way, my left arm steered me without the beating of the waves. I'd surface every fifty feet to gasp some air before diving under again.

Under the surface, I heard the familiar ticking of an outboard getting closer. My head lifted, and gunshots sounded from the yacht like small pops. I dove under again, kicking toward the yacht. When I surfaced again, I saw the boat I'd heard in the distance. A small fishing boat cut across the water from the north. The red and green navigation lights turned toward the yacht.

Without wasting another second, I continued swimming. The whir of the motor grew louder until it halted. I was within fifty feet of the yacht when I came up for air. The fishing boat bumped against the swimming platform. A black-haired Latino climbed onto the platform and pulled a gun from his side.

It occurred to me that the G36 sank with the airboat. I reached down to my belt, realizing the Glock 19 I'd taken off the Zebra in the Glades was no longer on my waist. It must have fallen out when I fell overboard.

When everything falls apart, improvise.

The man stepped over the transom, and I sank below the surface with a lungful of air. I swam up under the boat and came up behind the boat. The boat's name was *L'étoile,* which might have meant anything to me. For some reason, the word "celery" came to me. Somehow, I doubted anyone named their yacht after a vegetable. But people are strange. Still, if *L'étoile* was French, I knew nothing worth repeating in French.

Pushing the thought out of my mind, I heaved my body up onto the swim platform. The bow line which secured the fishing boat to the transom stretched as the wind pushed the little boat away from *L'étoile*. I straightened up to see the black-haired biker's back. I winced when he fired the gun.

The man muttered something in Spanish and stalked into the cabin of the boat. I was feeling naked without a weapon. Add in the useless arm, and the smart move would be to take the fishing boat and beat it to shore.

It might be the wisest action, but hell would freeze over before I left Caleb and his daughter in these people's hands. I stepped over the transom. The biker skulked forward with a Smith & Wesson forty-five aimed ahead of him. He stepped past two bodies. One fit the generic description of a *Las Serpientes* member. The other one had very little face to recognize. Someone shot both men point blank. A Beretta Px4 lay on the deck. I reached down and snatched it up in my left hand.

The biker was moving toward the lower level where the cabins should be.

"You are a tough bastard," the biker called to someone. "You can't last long. What did I hit? A lung? Maybe more. I can stand here and wait until you bleed out. Bet your daughter will love watching that."

"Hey asshole," I shouted, raising the Beretta and squeezing the trigger.

The man dropped down the stairs before the gun fired. He came up firing the forty-five, and

I dove behind an L-shaped sofa as I fired two more rounds forward. I tried to remember how many rounds the Beretta held. It should have a clip of at least nine rounds. How many had been shot before I picked it up? At least one.

Best-case scenario—five rounds. Worst case—well, I can throw the gun at him. If it was my gun, I'd judge it from the weight, but I hadn't held a Beretta in a long time.

"You're the other asshole that burned down my club?" the biker asked.

"Guilty," I answered. "Why don't you come on over here and let's settle that now?"

"I'll come fuck you up," he shouted back.

"That's not polite," I reprimanded. "You guys invited us to the party. It's not our fault you can't handle the hell we brought with us."

"It was just a damned car," the man spat.

"The hell it was," I corrected. "It was everything to those two."

"It was just some kids trying to make their place," he explained, as if that made everything just dandy.

"Oh, so not your fault, huh?"

"Fuck you," he blurted out.

"You the leader?" I asked. "What did that kid call you? Xavier?"

"Yeah, and I'm going to kill you both."

"Xave, can I call you that?"

"No, asshole," he said.

"Xave, you got nothing," I informed him. "Even if you walk away from this, the cops have your man. Gaspar. He doesn't strike me as the smartest bulb, but even he has to know if he rolls on you and the club, he might avoid the needle."

"There's no club left," Xavier admitted.

"Good," I retorted. "I'll give you one chance. You can throw your gun over here, and I'll let you make a run for it on your little boat. If you don't stop except for gas, you might make Cuba in a couple of days."

"Or I just kill you and Daddy in there. I've already gotten paid for the girl once. I can do it again."

"Shame you won't be around long enough to enjoy that money," I taunted.

A gunshot boomed in the cabin, followed by a slump of a body against the deck. As I stood up, I kept the Beretta at the ready.

"Clear," Caleb announced.

I stepped around to see the man leaning against the bulkhead in the corridor before sliding to the deck. Blood oozed from his back. The back of Xavier's head was a bloody mess.

"Shit," I exclaimed as I ran down to Caleb Saunders.

A blond-haired girl stared at me from the cabin next to her father. I looked at her, letting my face shift into a strained smile.

"Are you Amanda?" I asked.

She nodded.

"Okay, I need you to stay where you are, okay?"

"Are you going to hurt my daddy?" she asked.

"No, sweetie. He's my friend. I need to help him, though."

"Baby," Caleb muttered weakly. "Do what Chase tells you, please?"

"'Kay," she agreed.

"Just stay in here for right now," I told her as I pulled the door closed.

"I've lost a lot of blood," he admitted.

"I see that," I replied. "The resale value on this boat just plummeted."

My left arm slipped around his torso, hooking under his left armpit. "Let's get you into the galley. I'll see if I can patch you up this time."

As I lifted him, my legs muscles did most of the work. Once he was on his feet, he shuffled up the steps until got to the galley where I helped him down to the floor. I grabbed a roll of paper towels and used a wad to stuff against the entry wound.

"Looks like it didn't exit," I told him.

"Awesome," he mumbled.

"Don't move," I ordered.

He blinked at me.

"Yeah, yeah," I replied to his silent sarcasm. After several seconds of pulling open drawers and cabinets, I found a pair of poultry shears, a filet knife, a couple of metal skewers, and a bottle of vodka.

"I need to find something to close the wound," I explained. "Otherwise, pulling the bullet out won't help you much."

"Take your time," he quipped weakly. "I'm not going anywhere."

When I came up empty on the bridge, I rushed below to the head where, under the sink, I found a first aid kit. Most offshore cruisers have a suture kit, but *L'étoile* had the new zipper kind that works like an adhesive. It almost resembles a stencil of an accordion with a pull tab down the middle. I carried the entire kit back to the galley. On the way past, I peeked in on Amanda.

"Doing okay?" I asked.

She nodded demurely. I gave her a thumbs-up before shutting the door. It occurred to me the signal might have been more positive than it should be. I was never much of a field medic, and if the bullet damaged something vital, there might be little I could do to help Caleb.

"You ready for this?" I asked when I returned.

"Not especially," he answered as I laid out the tools I had.

"I have to get the bullet out," I explained as I ripped the tape holding my right arm up. I was going to need the extra hand to work on him.

He nodded.

"I don't have anything great for probing your innards, so bear with me."

"Do it," he commanded.

Before I started, I rinsed the two skewers with vodka. I ignited the front eye of the stove and let one of the metal sticks lay across the flame. If I had a bleed, it could theoretically cauterize everything it touched. As much as I didn't want to do it, I was more than a little grateful I was on this side of the procedure.

With the other skewer, I dipped the point into the bullet hole slowly. I didn't want to cause more damage. The angle the round took went down. Since there was no exit wound, I figured it was stuck on a rib. That was bad if it punctured a lung, but good if that was all the damage it did. However, it must have grazed a vessel given how much blood he was losing.

The metal end was almost six inches in when I felt it scrape something. It could have been bone, but I didn't think so. There was still no way to get it out. I wanted to roll him over and smack him a few times to dislodge it. It was deep enough that I would need to cut into him to actually get it out. I had nothing small enough to fit in the wound that was long enough to reach the bullet.

"I think I found it," I told him.

"It feels like you have your whole fist in there," he moaned.

"Not yet," I told him. "We have two choices here."

"Give them to me," he responded.

"I can leave the bullet inside you and cauterized everything," I explained. "At least I might could stop the bleeding."

"And the other option?"

"I can cut you open and dig the damned bullet out. I don't have great tools, but on the plus side, it will probably kill you."

"Is the bullet going to kill me?" he asked.

"Hell if I know," I answered. "Probably. Just maybe not right away."

"Close me up," he ordered.

"Okay," I agreed, reaching to the stove for the skewer, which was glowing red now. "Sorry, brother."

The bright red metal stick sizzled the flesh as it slid into the bullet hole. I had to move quick so that I could pull it out while it was still hot.

When the probe came out, I sighed. "It's over," I told him.

He didn't respond. I moved to check on him. He'd passed out, probably from the pain. But he was still breathing.

The suture set fit over the wound, and I pulled the tab which pulled the wound closed and stripped the adhesive cover off at the same time. The bullet hole was closed. So far, I wasn't seeing any more blood. After applying some antibacterial cream, I covered the wound with gauze to protect it.

If both of my arms were up to full strength, I'd have carried him down to the cabin to rest. Instead, I created a mat of pillows on the deck and rolled him into a nest on his side.

I went back down to check on the girl. She was curled up in a ball, fast asleep. Good, she can stay where she is.

It was almost two in the morning by now. I scoured through the galley. There was a half-gallon jug of orange juice. Caleb would need that when he woke up. It wasn't a saline drip, but it was a start.

The owner of the yacht had decent taste. I found some freshly sliced pancetta and pro-sciutto, which paired nicely with a half loaf of French bread. After I ate, I moved up to the bridge and checked the ship gauges. The fuel tank was full. According to the radar, the storm was almost done for the night. The western edge of the system would pass over us in a few minutes.

While the rain was still coming down, I dragged the three bodies out to the aft deck. Since I was somewhat shorthanded, it didn't matter how I treated them as I moved them. It took a little more effort to lift each of them up and drop them onto the swim platform. After that, it was a cinch to roll them into the sea.

There was still a blood trail leading from the cabin, but at least if Amanda came out, she wouldn't see any bodies.

"Chase?" I heard Caleb call out.

"You're back with me," I noted.

"It hurts like hell," he mumbled.

"What does?"

"Everything," he replied as I helped him sit up.

"Here, start drinking," I ordered, handing him a glass of juice.

"They're going to come after me," he told me.

"How do you feel?"

"Shitty," he remarked.

"But you could fight if you had to?"

He nodded.

"You don't have to," I assured him. "But you have a full tank of gas. Can you drive a boat?"

"I can figure it out," he admitted.

"As long as you don't go full speed, you could stretch the fuel to Mexico," I informed him.

He stared at me. "I can speak Spanish," he confessed.

THIRTY-FOUR

T he day was far too pretty for a funeral—let alone a quadruple funeral.

But Chase stood in the only black suit he owned next to Jay Delp. The four caskets were being interred at the Mount Carmel Cemetery just outside Raleigh, North Carolina. Audrey Harrod's parents wanted their daughter's family close to them. Even if only two of the caskets were full.

When Jay picked me back up at the same muddy embankment the next day, he brought a small army of law enforcement officers, including a replacement for Hubbard and Vickers, who turned out to be the Zebra that Caleb saved me from. Apparently, that was a coup on its own. The Office of Compliance never made an official appearance. I never got the name of the new Homeland Security agent, but he didn't seem convinced that Caleb and his daughter were lost in the storm.

"You're saying he had his daughter when he left in the airboat?" the agent questioned me.

I nodded. "He was trying to get away."

Jay added, "Coast Guard found the boat. It was barely floating after flipping in the storm."

"Why would he go out in that storm?" the man asked.

We both shrugged. "I couldn't stop him," I argued, showing my wounded arm.

He took notes, and when Jay pointed out Vickers was one of their agents and attempted to kill not only me, but almost succeeded with his own partner. After a quick phone call, he vanished for a bit.

The cops and National Park Service cleaned up what was left of the bodies. Apparently, after we left, the gators thought the two men made a decent dinner. They picked up the woman in the boathouse, too. She and Gaspar Castro seemed to be the only remaining members of *Las Serpientes*. At least that had shown themselves yet. From what the cops said, there was no great cultural loss with the demise of the motorcycle gang. So far, the suspected leader, Xavier Jimenez, was missing. It was presumed he was on the run after watching his club burn.

Now, we listened as one of Audrey Harrod's friends sang a tearful rendition of "I Will Always Love You." Given the woman's soft Appalachian twang, I figured it was the Dolly version, at least as far as everyone here was concerned. She had a beautiful voice. It was touching that Audrey was so loved.

"Just so you know," Jay whispered. "Please don't sing at my funeral."

Without cracking a smile, I retorted, "I won't. I have an interpretive dance prepared for it."

He shook his head solemnly.

"Where is he?" Jay asked under his breath.

"As far as we know, he's somewhere at the bottom of the Gulf."

"Pretty tragic," he admitted.

I wondered if he was being tongue in cheek or commenting on the life of Caleb Saunders.

A figure stood back by the trees.

"Is that your agent?" I asked.

Jay twisted his head to glance back. "Sure is. Agent Hubbard."

"She owes you her life," I pointed out.

He shrugged. "She's good people," he told me.

"Have you talked to her again?"

"Once. She's pissed someone else tried to take over her investigation."

I couldn't hide my smile. "You like her," I noted.

"She's something."

A little chuckle escaped my lips. "She going to be the next Mrs. Delp?"

"Flash," he scolded in a serious tone.

When Audrey's friend finished, everyone bowed their heads as the minister offered another prayer over the lives we were celebrating. It's one of those terms I despise. A celebration of life. Sometimes it fits—when we lay to rest a ninety-year-old woman with fifty grandkids and great-grandkids. But when the life belongs to a young boy barely into his life, it's not exactly something to celebrate. It should be rage-inducing. Jackson Harrod wouldn't be the last kid to be gunned down because some worthless shithead had something to prove. It wasn't some war-torn country; it was South Florida. He wasn't in the wrong place. He was with his family. Pumping gas because he wanted to be grown up like his dad. It angered me in the pit of my stomach.

When the prayer ended, the minister offered a few more inane words of comfort. Most of the time, the grieving are too numb to know or understand what is said. Abruptly, he ended his eulogy with an offer to meet in the church to share a repast with the family. He actually used the word "repast."

The crowd broke up. I considered moving toward the family to offer the slightest of relief, but I restrained myself.

"Detective Delp," the agent greeted blandly. I forced back a smile. She obviously liked him, too.

"Agent Hubbard," he replied.

"Geez, you two," I quipped.

Jay cut his eyes to me while Hubbard stared blankly at me.

Finally, she asked, "Can we go somewhere to talk?"

"All of us," I clarified, "or just the two of you."

Her head cocked in a warning to watch the level of crap I was dishing out. It wasn't a look that worried me, and if the Corps didn't beat it out of me, a simple Homeland Security agent sure wasn't going to—even if she worked for the clandestine assassin office.

"We were going to get some food," Jay suggested.

"Let's do a rain check," she replied. "I have to get back to D.C."

We moved toward another black Lincoln.

"How is the injury?" Jay asked.

"Healing slowly. If it hadn't been my partner shooting me, my career might be in the toilet."

"About that?" I asked.

"About that. I can't talk," she interjected. "But I have things to ask you."

"Such as?"

"Where is Caleb Saunders?" she asked.

I shook my head. "The last time I saw him, he left that embankment with his daughter."

"I didn't see any child there," she pointed out.

"Well, you were pretty busy getting shot and almost fed to alligators," I suggested. "You might have been too busy."

"How did she get out there?" Hubbard asked.

"One of the biker gang was running from us. We chased him down. We think the girl jumped off the boat about the time your partner tried to run us down." I was sure to add the part about Vickers. It seemed that was one area of the investigation no one wanted to talk about.

"So no one saw him leave but you?"

"Since Jay left to rush you to the hospital, yes. It was just me."

"Why would he run?" she asked.

"I don't know," I responded. "Why are you chasing him?"

No answer. Just another stoic stare.

"I don't think he's dead," Hubbard acknowledged.

"I'm sure that would be nice. The family would love to hear there's some hope."

Again with the silence.

"Unfortunately, my boss wants Saunders brought in."

"Or killed?" I clarified.

"Brought in."

"It would be interesting to hear all the stories Corsair has to tell, wouldn't it?" I asked.

"It wouldn't incriminate me," she advised, and I couldn't help but smile.

"If I can help, I will let you know," I told her. "Can I just reach you through Jay?"

She whipped out a business card and handed it to me. "My cell phone is there."

I took the card. "Are you sure you can't grab a bite?"

"I have a flight at two," she explained.

"Enough time for a burger on the way to the airport," I commented. "In fact, why don't you and Jay go? I'll meet you back at the hotel, Jay."

I took the rental car keys out of my pocket and rushed away, leaving the two of them alone. Jay didn't hurry to follow me, partly because he wanted to talk to Hubbard a little longer.

In the Nissan Sentra we picked up from Hertz, I turned on the radio and drove out of the cemetery. I wondered what was being offered at the repast. Funeral food in the South is usually good. But I didn't want to eat right now.

Instead, I drove south until I passed a small amusement park called Pullen Park where I took a right on Barbour Road and drove half a mile. The self-storage place was on the corner of Barbour and Blair. After the last self-storage, I was relieved to find this one actually seemed to operate solely for storage. There was a key code to get in. The unit was easy to find. 5-B. I removed the lock with a cordless Dremel. The cutting blade sliced through the hasp like butter.

Inside the unit, someone stacked furniture and boxes up. The smell of mothballs wafted past me. The first green lamp was not quite in the middle of the unit. I smashed the bottom. A plastic bag filled with cash fell out of the bottom. The matching lamp was on the other side of the unit. I repeated the process of breaking the bottom. Six passports fell out. I grabbed the IDs and cash, rolled them up tight, and dropped them in a USPS prepaid box.

As I left the unit, I closed it up and replaced the lock with an identical one. I blew a puff of air out to scatter the metallic dust away from the door. A forensic team could identify it, but there should be no reason for one to look here. Besides, I doubt it was uncommon for locks to be cut here.

Back in the Sentra, I drove northeast until I reached a Marriott Hotel. In front of the hotel was a blue mailbox. I walked to the box and opened the chute. With a final glance at the package, I read the address in Galveston, Texas, before I dropped it in. The chute creaked as it closed.

I walked back to the Sentra and headed to the Comfort Inn, where Jay and I were staying.

Also By Douglas Pratt

CPSIA information can be obtained
at www.ICGtesting.com
Printed in the USA
BVHW032222240423
662923BV00005BB/57